WONDER WHEELS

A NOVEL BY LEE BENNETT HOPKINS

ALFRED A. KNOPF · NEW YORK

WONDER WHEELS is a work of fiction. All names, characters and events are fictional, and any resemblance to real persons or actual events is unintentional.

THIS IS A BORZOI BOOK PUBLISHED BY ALFRED A. KNOPF, INC.

1   3   5   7   9   8   6   4   2
Library of Congress Cataloging in Publication Data.
Hopkins, Lee Bennett. Wonder wheels. Summary: The relationship of a star of the local roller rink and a sensitive girl from a neighboring town comes to an abrupt and tragic end. [1. Roller skating—Fiction] I. Title. PZ7.H7754Wo 1979 [Fic] 78–11774 ISBN 0–394–84125–5 ISBN 0–394–94125–X   pbk.

WONDER WHEELS—it's where the roller skating action is after dark.

Mick Thompson is the rink's star. Spinning, leaping, never missing a beat, he lives for the thrill of skating.

Kitty Rhoades watches from the sidelines. Her quiet strength and sweetness draw Mick to her. Soon every "Couples Only" is theirs together.

Mick's complacent world is suddenly jarred by a glimpse of Kitty's life which is as precarious as his is secure. As their relationship grows, Kitty shares her problems with Mick—all except one.

Just before the big skating competition, a sudden, tragic event uncovers a puzzling romantic triangle —Kitty's one secret. Mick is then left to work things out alone.

Wonder Wheels is a story of teenagers caught up in a world of motion—a bittersweet love story, bolstered by dreams and shattered by reality.

1

"MICK! IT'S TEN AFTER SEVEN! I'm not going to call you again. Get up! Now!"

"*Grr-rrr,*" he muttered into the pillow. "*Gr-rrr, grr-rrr, gr-rrr!*"

"Are you getting up? I'm not going to call you again, Mick. It's ten after seven. You wanted to get up at seven o'clock sharp and you've already spent ten extra minutes in that bed. Get up! Now! Or you're going to be late."

"I'm up!" he called, muttering a few more *gr-rrr's* and adding to himself, "At least I'm halfway up."

Mick and mornings never got on well. He hated getting up. He had always hated getting up. He especially hated getting up on Monday mornings.

"Are you up?" his mother called again. "I'm coming in whether you're up or not. I have to finish straightening up by seven thirty."

"I'm up," he grumbled, finally sitting up in the bed.

"Well, good morning," she said, coming into his room, holding the vacuum cleaner hose in one hand, dragging the vacuum with the other.

"I hate mornings!" he exclaimed. "There's *nothing* good about them."

"I know the feeling. You're not alone. But get up! Come on, please? I've got to straighten up this house by seven thirty," she repeated, plugging in the vacuum cleaner.

"What's so special about seven thirty?" Mick asked. "Going somewhere?"

"I foolishly agreed to be at Mrs. Raskin's house by eight thirty for a meeting about this year's used-book booth at the hospital fair. If I had known Mrs. Raskin called meetings for eight thirty in the morning—any morning—I wouldn't have volunteered."

"Can I ask you a foolish question?"

"What?"

"Why do you have to vacuum now?"

"Because I always vacuum on Monday. I want to get it over with so I don't have to do it when I come home this afternoon. Now do me a favor—jump into the shower and come alive. Try the new soap I bought yesterday. It's called Peppy. See if it lives

4

WONDER WHEELS

up to its name. Peppy! Imagine naming a soap Peppy. Does your store carry it yet?"

"I haven't seen it."

"That place is always the last to get the new items."

"I'll complain to Murph. I'll tell her Foods-For-You is losing customers 'cause it doesn't have Peppy. Murph'll really blow her mind on that! She'll have Carmen in for a half-hour meeting and threaten to fire him for 'not keeping up with consumer demands.' Sometimes Murph can be as mean as hell."

"Everybody's mean as hell sometimes. Like now. Look at you. You're a sorry sight in the morning," she said, pushing the vacuum cleaner back and forth under the dresser.

"Mom, can't you at least wait till I get out of bed? That noise is driving me crazy. Don't do under the bed, please? I don't want you to knock my skate box around. You'll dent it with that thing."

"Then why leave it under the bed? Why don't you put it in the closet when you come home? Look, I have to vacuum under your bed, so get up and move it. And the skates, too. Did you have a good time at Wonder Wheels last night?"

"It was O.K. The rink is really too crowded on Sunday nights. I like it better during the week when it isn't so packed. You could barely move there last night."

"You'd better move this minute or you're never going to get to work on time. Jump in the shower and let Peppy make you come alive. The minute you start to lather it's supposed to make you feel peppy all over. At least that's what the dumb ads say."

"Nothing could make me feel peppy all over at seven o'clock on Monday morning," he replied. "No thing!"

"It's not seven o'clock anymore. It's ten after. No —it's seven *fifteen* now. Get up!"

As he got out of bed and made his way into the bathroom, he heard her mutter, "Housework! Bah!"

Looking into the mirror, his eyes still filled with sleep, his hair a wretched wrangle of tangles, Mick laughed, thinking, "How in the hell can someone as handsome as me look so bad in the morning? *Grr-grr!*"

It must be seven twenty now, he thought. Ten minutes to perform miracles. Peppy soap never met such a challenge.

"It didn't pep me. At least I don't think it did," he said as he walked into the kitchen.

"Well, at least you smell good."

"Mom," Mick asked, going to the refrigerator for some orange juice, "what time did Dad leave this morning?"

"Early. He caught the six thirty train. He had an early meeting planned and wanted to review some notes. He told me to tell you he'll drive you to Wonder Wheels tonight if you want."

Mick laughed.

"What's so funny about that, may I ask?"

"It's Monday," he answered, smiling. "The rink is closed on Monday—every Monday. He should know that by now."

"He probably forgot. I forgot. And just for the record your father has more on his mind than keeping track of when Wonder Wheels is opened and closed. Finish your juice."

Mick downed the glass of orange juice. "What's the temperature?" he asked.

"I don't know," Jessica replied.

"Didn't you just see the weather report?"

"I didn't see it, I listened to it."

"So?"

"So by the time that man and his weather cartoons got through with all those highs and lows and airfronts and Celsius readings, I was completely confused and didn't care anymore. The only way I can tell what the weather is really like is to open the window and look! It must be about eighty. It's going to be another hot day."

"Gotta move," he said. "If I'm late old lady Murph will give me one of her looks. One of her looks means *beware!* More than one look kills you dead

7

on the spot, or at least you wish you were. I should be home about six thirty. See you at supper. Have fun at Mrs. Raskin's," he added, laughing.

"Mrs. Raskin is as much fun as falling down a flight of stairs."

"You know what? You're pretty rotten in the morning, too," he joked.

"Thanks. Nothing like a nice compliment from a loved one so early in the morning."

"You know I'm kidding. 'Bye, Mom."

" 'Bye, and have a good day," she said, giving him a kiss on his chin.

Mick took a funny mock bow and then hurried off to work.

2

"GOOD MORNING, MURPH," Mick called up as he headed for the time clock.

"Morning. Have a nice weekend?"

"Weekend? I had a nice yesterday," he answered. "I was here until seven o'clock on Saturday."

"One day off is enough for anybody," Murph said. "I don't know why companies ever gave in to the five-day workweek. Six days keeps people out of trouble, particularly in these times when trouble is so easy to come by."

Mick thought but wouldn't dare say, "To each her own!"

Murph literally lived in Foods-For-You. She didn't have to, but she had worked Monday through Saturday every week for the past twenty years. Her job was her life. She was Miss Brutal! For kicks she took everyone's time card home on Saturday night and studied them all day Sunday. If anyone was even a minute late for work or back from lunch, she'd let them know about it on Monday morning, making them make the time up. She hovered over the store as if she owned it and all its chains. She had no family, never talked about friends, and when she wasn't doing her job as manager, she was busy working against the union, spending most of her time setting back work conditions for employees a hundred years.

"I'm glad to see you are six minutes early," she said from atop her office, which everyone called Murph's Throne. "You've got a good time record. Keep it up and you might win the summer part-time help award. That's one of the biggest honors we give here."

"Great," Mick wanted to say. "Just what I need. A supermarket part-time help award!" Aloud he asked, "Where's Andy?" He picked out Andy's time card from the steel slot. "I see he's in too."

"He's downstairs. Tell him to get up here as soon as he can. I want him to open up on time. Eileen's already counting her drawer."

"Right, Murph," Mick answered.

"When you're dressed, check in with Carmen. I want you to do price changes this morning."

As he walked away from the Throne he called to Eileen, who was busily cracking packages of coins into her drawer. "Hi, Eileen. How are you doing?"

"Hi, Mick. How are you?"

"Fine."

"Are you on register two today?"

"No, Andy is. I'm doing p.c.'s."

"Well, there goes my Monday," she said. "I thought I'd have a chance to stare at that yummy body of yours. Anyone ever tell you you're prime-choice stuff?"

"Yeah, everyone!" he answered.

There was a time when a remark about his looks or body would have sent him up a wall. But he became used to people telling him how good-looking he was and decided to just take it all in stride; accept the compliments and not let it go to his head.

"See you later," he said to Eileen. He pushed open the door leading downstairs to the locker room.

Once he was wide awake and at work, Mick enjoyed the feeling of the store on Monday mornings. It had the same quiet-stillness about it that Wonder Wheels had when it was empty. He liked the quiet store especially after Saturday, when customers lined up constantly from 8:30 right until the bell sounded at 6:00 to let people know the store was about to close.

The store was never busy on Monday morning. Yet a funny kind of chaos encompassed it, the result of the weekend horde that had stormed through. On Mondays, only two cashiers checked out groceries most of the day. Eileen, who had been working at Foods-For-You for fifteen years, always got the express lane, checking out customers with twelve items or less. She was a demon at the register. Her fingers rang up prices faster than most customers could get the products on the conveyor belts. She prided herself on the fact that she never made a mistake. Her cash drawer was always perfect, right down to the penny. She also prided herself on the fact that she was Miss Seniority—she had every Saturday off.

Andy was given next priority; one, because of his partly-crippled leg, and two, because Murph adored him. He was the only person in the store she did like. And he was the only one who could make her smile. That was a feat unto itself.

If things did get busy on a Monday, Murph would bellow over her loudspeaker for Mick or Carmen, the full-time stock boy who subbed at the checkout, to open up a register. Greg and Sandra, who worked part-time like Mick, were off on Mondays, so things were extra quiet.

Mondays were spent stocking and leveling out the shelves—placing newer items to the back, putting older ones up front—and doing price changes. Mick liked doing p.c.'s. It gave him an opportunity to talk with some of the regular customers while they pushed their carts up and down the aisles. He especially looked forward to seeing Bargain Gertie, one of the most colorful characters.

Every Monday morning, Bargain Gertie would come into the store to buy a quart of milk and a loaf of discounted bread left over from Saturday. That's all she ever bought—but it wasn't all she got from Foods-For-You.

Bargain Gertie would walk up and down each and every aisle, hunting damaged packages. If a package of cookies was opened, Bargain Gertie would reach in, munch on a couple; if candy was unwrapped, she'd take a few pieces from the bag, eat them, and stuff a few more into her pocketbook.

Her favorite pastime was passing by the produce aisle and picking up damaged fruit and vegetables. Al, the produce manager, would pack them up for her in a bag marked *No Charge*. Although Al had been doing this for her for years, she always played the same game with him. And he loved it.

"Whatcha got for Gertie today?" she'd ask.

Al would show her some of the stuff he had to throw out. She'd study each piece, looking at it as carefully as a woman would look over diamonds in Tiffany's.

Occasionally she'd let out a grunt to reprimand Al. "Should be ashamed to sell this garbage," she'd tell him. "You gonna charge me for this garbage? Ain't right. If I reported you to the Board of Health, you'd lose your job. They'd close this whole place down, that's what they'd do. I know someone who works at the Board of Health, you know. Someone in an important position. Gertie has a lot of good friends in high positions. Lots of 'em."

"Pick out what you need," Al always told her. "I'll give it to you for no charge."

Then, smiling through her loose and yellowed front teeth, she'd laugh and laugh, while continuing to study a bruised tomato or too-ripe banana. She'd end up taking whatever she could, handing it over to Al. He'd put it in a bag and no-charge mark it with his black felt-tip pen.

"Thanks to you, Al. You're a good man. The likes of you ain't around no more. You've always been good to me, and when old Gertie goes, she's gonna leave you somethin' in her will. I'll leave you somethin' special. You'll see."

Then, taking a pencil stub from her bag, she'd walk over to the scale, weigh the goods, and write something down on a pad she carried that looked as old as she was.

"Gotta keep my records straight, you know. Gotta know how much you gave me this week."

When she finished with Al she'd make her way to Eileen's register, stopping to chat with her and always showing her the bag of produce Al gave her. After paying for the bread and milk, she'd go out of the store. No one saw her again until the following Monday.

Mick became fond of Bargain Gertie in the short time he'd been at Foods-For-You. Today, after munching her way down the cookie aisle, she stopped when she saw him.

"Whatcha doin'?" she asked.

"Price changes," he answered.

"Makin' everythin' higher, I bet. They never do no price changin' to make things lower, do they? Only higher and higher. Higher and higher. Soon we won't be able to afford no eatin' of nuthin'. Greedy—that's what everyone is. Plain greedy. I remember payin' one slim dime for milk when I was a young one. Now it's sixty-two cents. Sixty-two cents for somethin' that used to cost one slim dime. Over six times higher. Ain't no justice."

Rapidly changing the subject, she asked, "What's a good-lookin' kid like you doin' in a dump like this anyhow? Huh? You should be on TV or somethin'. 'Stead of makin' food prices higher. You sing or dance or somethin'?"

"No," Mick answered, embarrassed, but also taken by the character she was.

"Do anythin'?"

"I skate."

"Skate? On ice?"

"No, I roller-skate. Roller skating's my thing, Gertie."

"Ain't much room for roller skatin' on TV. Ya don't see much of that. TV's too small for skatin.' You want to go on TV? With your looks you'd be a hit. A big hit. You're prettier than that Donny and Marie. You let Gertie know if you want to go on TV. I've got lots of important friends who work on TV. I'll talk to them 'bout ya. They listen when Gertie talks.

"Gotta go now. Gotta buy some fresh vegetables. Monday's a good day to buy fresh. That's why I come here on Monday. No other reason I'd come to this dump. See ya next week," she said.

Mick smiled as she pushed her completely empty shopping cart down the aisle.

"How's it coming?" Carmen asked, carrying a case of coffee.

"O.K.," Mick answered.

"When you finish this, do the soup. Here's the list. They're on special this week—three for a buck with a coup."

Coups! Store coupons drove the cashiers into a frenzy. Some days Mick had almost as many coupons in his register drawer as he did cash. Seven cents off on this, a dime off on that. And all the different shapes and sizes of the coupons took up too much room in the register drawer. The cashiers were convinced that whoever started coupons did it just to drive them crazy.

One quickly learned Murph's rules-of-the-coupons, especially checking expiration dates, or it was all over. And no one was dumb enough not to check if a customer handed them one for a product Foods-For-You didn't carry. Murph knew every single product in the entire store—from Mrs. Goodman's Matzoh Ball Soup to Peter's Perfect Piccalilli.

At times, Mick had a hard time figuring out customers. Most of them came through the checkout lane without saying a word, paying, picking up their bags, and leaving. But there were some who had peculiar habits.

Andy always dubbed them with great names— like Coupon Kid, Double-bag Bertha, and Grab-bags Bernie.

Mick met Coupon Kid the first week he was on the register.

"Beware!" Andy called over. "Coupon Kid's in your line. Check every coup carefully. He'll give you tons of them."

He did!

Coupon Kid, a slim, thirty-ish man, came in weekly, always alone, carrying a rectangular box with *My Coupon Collection* printed boldly on it in bright-colored letters. He had thousands of coupons stuffed into the box—coupons for just about everything, all organized and separated with a card marked by the aisles. It almost seemed as if he only bought items he had coupons for.

Double-bag Bertha, another character, insisted that a variety of items each be put into separate bags.

"Double-bag the frozen juices so they won't drip all over the artichokes. Double-bag the soap powder. I don't want it on my meat. Double-bag the tuna fish so I can find it easily. That's for my neighbor."

Before anything was double-bagged, she insisted that one bag be put into another bag so that the full package wouldn't fall apart.

The customer Mick thought was the funniest was Grab-bags Bernie. "I'll bag for you," he'd say, and while Mick was checking the groceries, he'd start packing things in a bag, grabbing bags galore from the counter, quickly folding them in half and shoving them down the side of the bag he was bagging!

By the time he was through, he had taken ten or twenty bags. Mick wondered what he did with them.

Aside from the regulars, and characters like these, who Andy and Eileen knew from working there so long, no one knew anyone's name—or cared. They were just nameless people who drifted in and out of the supermarket through a small lane with a conveyor belt.

Mick thought about this at times. He wondered about the many people who drifted in and out of his life. Other than his mom and dad, and a few good friends from the rink, everyone else was just an acquaintance or a passing face, going by in one given moment in time.

He didn't even know about the people he worked with, other than information gathered from bits and pieces of conversation he picked up from talking with them. No one had anything in common with anyone. If he hadn't met people like Andy and Eileen and Murph at he store, they too would be just passing faces, that is if he even noticed they were alive.

3

MICK COULDN'T STOP THINKING about the store customers and the other faceless faces who seemed to
be passing through his life at a more rapid pace
than ever.

"You know, Dad, the older I get the more I think
that everyone is like a horse on a merry-go-round.
You know what I mean?" he said one night after
dinner.

"Not exactly," his father replied.

"What I mean is, like when you're a kid and go
to an amusement park, it seems that almost everything goes around and around—the Ferris wheel,
the caterpillar, the whip—most rides just go around
and around and around and you never know what
car you're in or what horse you're on. They're just
there, constantly going around and around. People
are like that sometimes to me. Like the customers at

the store. They come in day after day, week after week, pushing carts up and down the aisles like they're in a giant maze, ending up at the register, going out the door and coming back at another time, going up and down again, like merry-go-round horses or cars on a Ferris wheel."

"That's a good analogy," his father said. "I know what you mean. But so what? You can't know everyone who passes through your life. Life *is* a merry-go-round. You hit it right on the horse's hoof, kid. It's all one big hell of a merry-go-round. Be happy that you know a few people real well—people that you want to know real well. You really want to know half the creeps you tell us about who shop at the supermarket?"

"No, but sometimes I'd like to know more about some of them—like Bargain Gertie. Who she really is, where she lives, *how* she lives, how she manages. I don't even know her name."

"You just said her name was Bargain Gertie."

"That's just a name Andy gave her. She has to have a last name."

"Ask her."

"You don't ask people who shop in the store those kinds of questions. You don't ask them anything. Old Murph gets crazy if you talk to the customers."

"Before you're old and hoary you're going to meet plenty of horses on the merry-go-round. Zillions! You forget most of them. Even those you thought were important at one time in your life. It's the age of alienation and isolation. It's the merry-go-round generation in all its glory. Nobody gives a damn about anybody today. All they're interested in is themselves—*I, mine, I, me, mine*. It's harder today to know someone well. That's because when you start getting to know them well, you either wished you hadn't bothered, or they go away! Smack! Right out of your life. Another turn of the carousel."

Although he knew it was true, it didn't satisfy Mick. At times he yearned to know someone well— to share things with, to exchange thoughts and feelings. Someone to know more about and to care for. Someone other than just another passing face.

"What time are you leaving?" Mick's father asked, looking at his watch.

"About seven twenty," Mick replied. "J.P. should be here any minute. I told him to come at seven. Since he's never on time for anything, I figure he'll come over about ten past seven. It'll take him three minutes to find out what Mom made for dessert, one minute to tell her he really shouldn't eat it, another three minutes to devour it, and three minutes to get him out of the house. That'll be seven twenty—exactly!"

"You've got him down to the minute. He's a great guy, but I don't know how he stays so slim eating so much junk."

"Junk? Did I hear you say junk, David?" Jessica

asked, putting down a magazine, taking off her glasses. "Is that what you think of my desserts? You didn't seem to think the icebox cake was junk. You even had a second slice, dear, remember?"

"Whoa! That's *not* what I meant," David retorted. "I meant that whenever J.P. pops into the house, he's ready to pounce on one of your desserts."

"And they're junk?"

"You *know* that's not what I meant. I meant that he's always eating something sweet. Mick, tell Mom about J.P. and the Twinkies."

"I heard about J.P. and the Twinkies. Twinkies *are* junk. My icebox cake is *dessert*."

Mick smiled at them. "Did you two ever have a real knock-'em-down, tear-'em-up fight?" he asked.

"We never fight. We just argue once in a while," his mother said. "Speaking of socks—"

"Socks?" Mick asked puzzledly.

"Who said anything about socks?" his father asked.

"*I'm* speaking about socks," she replied.

"Oh, no!" his father exclaimed, doubling over with laughter.

"What's the matter with you two?" Mick asked.

Laughing, Jessica said, "We fought once. Over socks. Your dad didn't talk to me for about two hours."

"How did socks come into this conversation?" Mick asked.

"Yesterday when I did the laundry I noticed your skating socks were wearing out."

"What do my socks have to do with the joke, may I ask?"

"Tell him about the sock incident, David."

"I had to make an important speech one morning in Hartford, Connecticut," his father began. "Your mom decided to go with me. She packed the suitcase and forgot my socks. The next morning when I got up and started to get dressed, I couldn't find my socks."

"I forgot them," Jessica interrupted.

"Here I was, an hour to go before I was to make this really important speech to several hundred clients—and no socks."

"Why didn't you wear the socks you wore the day before?" Mick posed.

"I didn't wear any. It was in the middle of August and I wore sandals going up there."

"Well, what did you do?"

"He wasn't due at the meeting until ten o'clock," his mother said, taking up the story. "We got dressed and shot into downtown Hartford to find a pair. But the stores were on summer hours and didn't open up until ten."

"I needed to blame someone, so Jessica was *it!*" his father added. "I couldn't possibly go to the meeting in sandals. And I couldn't go sockless."

"We finally found a bargain store about a block

away that was opened." His mother smiled, remembering. "But the only socks they carried were bright green ones."

"Gardening socks," his father added. "The ugliest shade of lime green you ever saw. Here I was dressed in a brand new expensive white linen summer suit with patent-leather shoes—and she brings me this pair of bright green twenty-nine-cent socks."

"Thirty-nine cents. I'll never forget the price nor the look on your face when you took them out of the bag."

"The bag looked better," his father added. "I told her to go in and get another bag and I'd wear the bags on my feet! Well, we made the meeting on time but all through the morning I thought about those socks. As soon as the meeting was over and we got in the car, I took them off. We stopped at the nearest rest station and I threw them into the first trash container I saw."

"We should have saved them," Jessica said. "He didn't talk to me the whole way home."

"Mick! Mick! It's me, J.P. The screen door's locked again."

"Sweet tooth's here. I'll get it," Mick said. "Get the icebox cake ready. I'm only giving him three minutes to gobble it up. Hey, that's a funny story," he added. "You two are great."

"Yeah," his father said. "A perfect pair. Get it, Jessica? Pair? Like a pair of socks?"

"Got it, dear. But it's corny. Worse than the lime green socks!"

"Why do you want to get to the rink so early?" J.P. asked, starting up the car. "It doesn't open up till eight fifteen."

"Tonight's special. Ange told me the rules are being distributed tonight. I want to get them as soon as I can. Ange said he'd be there at seven thirty. I can't wait to see them."

"When do the auditions take place?"

"The last Saturday night in August.

"August? You'll have plenty of time to learn the rules."

"I know, but I'm anxious. This is a big deal, J.P. I really want to win. It'll take me a month to get everything together. I've been working on a new routine since last May when I first found out about the auditions from Ange. I've got to be perfect-plus. Ange says it's all over in a few minutes. I still have to practice my spins. And I still have to find the right music. Anything come in yet?"

"New records come in every day. Tons of them. I go through as many I can."

"I appreciate that, J.P. I'm counting on you. No one knows records like you do."

"I don't know why you won't use something from

the Backdoor Five album. They're great. It's been on top of the charts for eight weeks."

"That's why I don't want to use anything from it."

" 'Movie Queen in the Dark' is great stuff. You use it for practice, why not for the audition?"

"Because by the time the auditions come up, five or more people could use it. I have to find something perfect for the spins. 'Movie Queen' isn't right for that part of the routine. It slows down too fast at the end—at the *ser-eene* part. I know it isn't right. I can feel it. I want something fresh, smashing. Keep listening? Please?"

"You know I will. But Mr. Bergman, fathead owner himself, hates the sound of today's groups. He calls it 'discordant din.' It's his favorite phrase. Every time I put on a disk he gives me the same speech about today's youth being tone-deaf. Then I hear about the good old days of Bing Crosby and Frank Sinatra. The only new recording star he thinks is any good is Barbra Streisand—even though she's been around since before I was born. If I hear her sing 'People' one more time, I'll break the record. *She* hasn't heard it as many times as I have. Nor his story about that song *belonging* to him and his wife. If I hear him tell another living soul how he met his wife in the standing-room-only section at the Winter Garden Theatre when she played there —in *Funny Girl*—I'll break out in hives."

"I thought Barbra was your patron saint?"

"She was before this summer. You try listening to her albums day in and day out. *Nobody's* that good."

"How's the job coming along otherwise?"

"O.K. But I'll be glad when school goes back already. It's a lot easier going to school than working all summer in that record shop. I need a rest away from Bergman, Barbra, and the customers. You should be glad you're working in the supermarket. Cans are quiet."

"Cans are. But cash registers aren't. And neither are some of the customers. Mind if I plug in 'Movie Queen'? I want to run through the routine in my head. Just for practice."

"The cassette's in the glove compartment."

Mick opened the glove compartment, took out the cassette, and pushed it into the player. The music sounded throughout the car:

> *Movie Queen*
> *Feast your eyes on that flashing screen*
> *Colors fly*
> *Make you high*
> *Don't know why*
> *Your eyes stay dry*
> *When the colors fly*
> *Fly on by*
> *On the flashing screen—*

28

Flashing screen
Movie Queen
My, oh, my
You're so serene.

"See! That's where it goes wrong. I need something that doesn't end so abruptly. The music goes nowhere. Besides, the lyrics are stupid."

"Most lyrics are stupid. You listen to the music, not the words."

"Even the music is stupid. It slows down too much on that last line."

"So why don't you change the routine? You've plenty of time. Slow up with it."

"I can't, J.P. My spins are what make me good."

"Only in your mind. No matter what you do on skates you're great. You're the greatest thing on wheels since the invention of the car."

"Thanks, but you're prejudiced."

Everything is so ser-eene.

The cartridge stopped.

"What in the hell do they mean by 'so serene'?"

"Who?"

"The Backdoor Five. Those last few lines: *'My, oh, my, / You're so serene / Everything is so ser-eene.'* It doesn't make sense. The whole song doesn't make sense."

"That's why it's number one on the charts for eight weeks. The less sense it makes, the more people go for it. Nothing makes sense today. I told you people buy records for the sound, the music—not the lyrics."

"Maybe I should skate to 'People,'" Mick said jokingly.

"Go ahead. But find yourself another ride to Wonder Wheels. I'm 'People'd-out! Stop worrying so much about the music for your routine. There's music inside you. You not only have magic in your feet, you've got music in your head and heart. How can you lose?"

4

MICK AND J.P. WERE THE ONLY ONES Angelo let into the rink early. Angelo did a lot of special favors for Mick. He always had. Recently he allowed Mick to stay later at the rink so he could practice without anyone else on the floor, and he even let him lock up once in a while. He knew that Mick wasn't just another kid coming to the rink to fool around, the way so many of them did. Mick was a dedicated skater— something special on wheels.

Angelo had sensed this shortly after Mick started to come to the rink, and that was years ago. Mick's mother took him for the first time on his eighth birthday. From the minute he put skates on his feet he was completely hooked. For four years he took private lessons from Angelo. Angelo taught him everything he knew about skating—spins, sprints, springs, leaps, and a myriad of dance steps. He taught him how to choreograph each and every bar of music, not wasting even half a second to a beat.

Last April, when Angelo found that Paradise Lane, U.S.A., had definitely chosen Wonder Wheels as one of their audition sites, he called Mick at home to share the news and encourage him to audition.

Paradise Lane, U.S.A., a family-type entertainment park, was located in Yorktown Heights in New York's Westchester county. It was a small-scale version of the Disney parks in Florida and California, or Opryland in Nashville, Tennessee. During the summer months thousands of visitors from all over the country visited Paradise Lane. In addition to rides and other attractions, it had live spectacular shows. It was a showcase for new talent. Many performers went on to television, touring in road companies, or even making it on the Broadway stage. To be seen performing at Paradise Lane, U.S.A., meant you were good—very good.

The park employed about one hundred entertainers in six staged extravaganzas covering just about every phase of the music world, from Dixieland to salutes to Broadway. Auditions for young singers and dancers were held on college campuses in New York, New Jersey, and Pennsylvania.

Angelo had read that for the first time since Paradise Lane, U.S.A., had opened, it was planning a feature called "America on Wheels." He immediately contacted the park's manager urging him to hold auditions at Wonder Wheels. The invitation was accepted.

Angelo was really happy about this. Wonder Wheels would be one of only three audition sites. Only twelve skaters would be chosen from all three auditions—the one at Wonder Wheels, one at a rink in New York City, and one in Pennsylvania. Angelo knew it would spark business; it was like getting thousands of dollars worth of free advertising hopefully putting Wonder Wheels on the constantly growing map of roller-skating rinks.

The popularity of roller skating died out in the early 1960s. Angelo blamed television because in those years people just sat looking at the tube. But in the late 1970s, roller skating had a new burst of popularity. Angelo connected it with the onslaught of skateboards and disco dancing: skateboards put American feet back on wheels and disco dancing gave people a chance to enjoy themselves and let themselves go.

Business had picked up in the last few years, although it couldn't compare with the 1940s or early '50s. Then people had come in such great numbers that he had had to turn some of them away.

Another spark came in the late 1970s. For the first time, roller skating was included as part of the summer Pan American Games; there was the announcement that roller skating would be included in the 1980 Olympics.

Angelo was positive the auditions would boost business. And it was a chance for Mick to be seen by someone, possibly getting him star billing in the park's new show.

Mick didn't really care about getting star billing, but he wanted desperately to be one of the twelve chosen. It would provide him with a good job next summer, ensuring that he wouldn't have to return to Foods-For-You. Most important, he could do something he loved more than anything else in the world. He loved skating as much as he loved life.

"Ange," Mick shouted as he walked in the back door of the rink. His voice echoed through the empty hall.

"Up here," Angelo shouted back from the organ rise perched in the center of the rink. "I'm getting Rosemary's numbers together. Hi, J.P."

"Hi, Ange."

"Did the rules come in?" Mick asked anxiously.

"Naw," answered Angelo.

"Damn!" Mick bellowed. "You said they'd be in by tonight. If they don't come soon, how will anyone know what they want from us?"

"I know," Angelo answered.

"How do you know if you haven't seen them?"

As he came down the stairs from the organ rise,

Angelo was smiling. "I just happen to have a hundred copies in my office. That's how."

"But you said—"

"I was only teasing you. Thought I'd make your juices flow. Come into my office."

Mick and J.P. followed on Angelo's heels.

"Here's a copy for each of you. They'll be distributed tonight, and three copies will be posted around the rink. Don't lose 'em."

"Lose them?" Mick said, flipping through the five pages of stapled mimeographed papers. "I'll have them memorized before I get the chance to lose them."

"You and J.P. look them over. I've got to put some tickets in the box office."

Mick and J.P. walked to the nearest bench and plopped down.

"This is a lot to read," J.P. said. "And the print is so small. Hey, look at this—on page three. They give the pay rates."

"Don't get ahead of me. Let me read it from the beginning."

"You read it. The audition will be over before I could plow through all that. I'm going to put on my skates."

Mick began pouring through the rules.

PARADISE LANE, U.S.A., AUDITIONS
Read Thoroughly Before Auditioning

Thank you for your interest in Paradise Lane, U.S.A., auditions. The following information will answer many of your questions. Auditions will be held at Wonder Wheels Skating Rink on August 25th, at 8:00 p.m. *Sharp.*

We will be seeing a large number of people. In order to give each his/her opportunity, we ask that everyone be prepared in the following ways:

I. NEEDS

a) Fill out application *Completely.* Missing information could result in inability to notify you.

b) Audition is limited to approximately THREE minutes.

"J.P.," Mick called. "They only give you three minutes."

J.P. didn't answer.

c) Be prepared for audition including show skates, costumes, and a recording or tape of your selected music *or* prearranged music with an accompanist.

II. STANCE

a) First impressions are vital. A nice smile, pleasant personality, and personal appearance are important pluses when performing before judges.

Skating over to Mick, J.P. said, "You still on the first page?"

36

"There's a lot here that doesn't say anything. I'm on part three."

III. PERFORMING BEFORE JUDGES

a) Choosing the right music is one of the most important parts of your audition. Musical selections should demonstrate your particular talents to best advantage. Consider a tempo and theme variation that will best show your talent.

b) Don't be upset if asked to stop before finished. Many others must be seen and our good judges can tell what they need after your first few movements. *Remember:* Only twelve skaters will be chosen from all those seen in three skating rinks.

c) When your number is called for the first time . . .

"What do you think?" Angelo asked, walking over to Mick.

"I haven't gone through all this yet. It's long. So far there's nothing here that I wouldn't already have expected."

Seeing Rosemary walk into the rink, he called, "Hi, Ro."

"Hi, Mick. I see you have the rules. Ange just handed them to me. Long, aren't they?" she asked, flipping through her copy. "How come you don't have your wheels on? The vultures are already lined up at the door."

"I wanted to read this through."

"You've got over a month to do that."

"I know. But I want to read it."

"I don't know why you're so anxious about all this. You'll win. Mark my words."

"I've got a chance in a thousand."

"You'll win. When Rosemary says something, she means it. There hasn't been anyone on wheels around here like you in a mighty long time."

"Yeah, but what do you know about skaters in Pennsylvania and New York? There must be thousands of kids just as good—or better—than me."

"No, no, baby. You'll win. Toes down. Rosemary's betting on you. You're going to put Wonder Wheels on the map someday. I've seen plenty of skaters. Too many, come to think of it. Some are O.K., some good, some extra-good—but when you get on that floor and dance on your wheels, magic takes over. I've watched you develop for years. You've got what it takes, kid. I've been pumping that organ up there for longer than I care to think about. Haven't seen anyone who would compare to you. I'm telling you again, you're magic on wheels."

"Thanks, Ro. I wish I felt as confident about myself as you do."

"If you need to talk some steps out, don't hesitate to come to me. I've seen it all, kid. I've seen the worst and the best, and you're better than any best I've seen. You're in. You listen to me."

Rosemary was a fixture at Wonder Wheels. She

had played the organ at the evening sessions for thirteen years. Although she never skated, she did know skating—and she knew music. Her fingers were as magical on the organ keyboard as Mick's feet were on skates.

At the end of each night's session, competition skating was held. For some it was a chance to show off new steps, new routines. Some of the kids were dynamite on skates, like Lisa Wells who did ballet and Jingo Fernandez who tapped. Mick knew they'd both have a big chance of winning in the auditions. But he didn't care about that. They were both good friends of his.

What he couldn't know was that he was special on skates. His body radiated when he performed— jet black hair furling, flying at each turn, sinewy body slithering as if he were moving through air. His arms, hands, fingers, legs, and feet all said, "Look at this. I'm here. I'm a skater."

He was confident because he knew he was good, but nothing could allow him to capture the charisma he generated when he skated. He was perfection from head to toe. He was born to be on wheels.

The stream of skaters coming in changed the atmosphere of the rink. Minutes ago, the place seemed like an empty amusement park; the skate-rental concession was quiet, the vending machines in a lull waiting for customers to plunk in change to dispense Cokes, ice-cream bars, and Wonder Wheel paraphernalia—pom-pons for skate decorations, decals to stick on skate boxes, small pennants blaring *WONDER WHEELS—HOME OF THE BEST* in bright red and yellow letters.

The hardwood-maple skating arena gleamed, blaring its high polish, waiting to hold up the evening's weight of people rolling around and around.

"Lisa's here," J.P. said, skating over to Mick. "She's putting on her wheels. You should see her skirt. Dynamite! What legs she's got. Yum. I would even give up Twinkies for her. Hey! You still don't have your skates on? Read that crap later. Come on, Mick. Ro should be starting in a few minutes."

Mick looked down at the sheet of paper, picking up where he had left off.

c) ... please go to the center of the rink.
d) Finally, have confidence in your ability. Nervousness is expected, but be as relaxed as possible. Let your personality and talent be projected to their fullest.

IV. IF NOT SELECTED ...

"See you have the audition rules," Lisa interrupted. "I'm reading them tomorrow. How come you don't have your skates on?"

"Can't you see I am reading them *now*?"

"Read them later. Come on. Warm up with me. Can I have first Couples Only with you?"

40

"Sure. Don't you always?"

"Just thought I'd ask. I never take *anything* for granted, especially with you. Seen Jingo?"

"No."

"I've got news for you. He's not auditioning."

"What? Why?"

"He doesn't want to. He's working at his uncle's car wash next summer before going to college. He told me last week he'd do better there with tips and all than he would at some amusement park. I'm glad. That means we have a better chance of winning. Wouldn't it be great if we were *both* selected? We'd be able to spend all next summer together. I'm going to practice all summer until I collapse, if I have to."

"Yeah," Mick answered somewhat unenthusiastically.

Rosemary flashed on the bright rink lights, turned the card to *All Skate*, and began playing the organ. Within seconds the rink filled up.

"See you on the floor," Lisa said. "Remember, I've got first Couples Only with you."

"Hey, Lisa," Mick called as she skated away. "Your skirt is nice."

Lisa stopped short, smiled, and said, "Thanks, Mick. Glad you noticed."

Mick knew that remark would make her whole night. Although Lisa was a pain sometimes, he

41

didn't want to hurt her or make her feel he was always down on her.

He opened his skate box, took out his skates, and threw the sheets of paper into the box. He wanted to get on the floor.

5

"PRETTY, PRETTY!" JINGO CALLED, skating into the men's room where Mick was standing in front of the mirror combing his hair.

"Hi, Jingo," Mick said. "How come you're so late?"

"I'm not late. I was helping Chester at the skate-rent. He's busy tonight. Get the rules?"

"Yeah. Hey, Jing, Lisa told me you weren't auditioning for Paradise Lane. How come?"

"I'm going to work at my uncle's car wash next summer. I need the bread—badly! You see the rates they pay? I can make that without strain or pain at my unc's place. And I can save some bread by being at home. Besides, who has a chance with you in the competition?"

"Come on, Jing. Your routine's great."

"Yeah, if they're looking for a Puerto Rican tap dancer on wheels. I'm really not into it like you are. But I know you'll slay them. Their eyes will roll right out on the floor when you dance."

"You know, if I don't win I'll never be able to show my face here again? Why is everyone so sure I'll win?"

" 'Cause you will. Love that shirt. Pretty, pretty!"

"Mick," J.P. called, rolling into the men's room. "Hi, Jing. How's things?"

"Fine, J.P. Just fine. My things are bursting. After the rink closes tonight, me and Mary Lou are going to Pop's Pizza. Then afterward, who knows? The pepperoni just might send sparks through her bod. And I'll be ready!"

"You're always ready."

"That's right, man. The first time I get it I'm gonna hire an airplane and tell the whole world about it in skywriting."

The three of them laughed.

"Hey, Mick, I almost forgot. Lisa's looking for you. Couples Only is coming up," J.P. said.

"Let's go," said Jingo. "Gotta find my Mary Lou. *Whoo-whoo-whoo!* Mick, let's you and me and Lisa do the Trio."

"You're on," Mick said. "I'll tell her to meet us at the Coke machine."

"Great. See you later."

Rosemary pushed the light board to darken the

44

hall and start the strobe globe spinning. She then put up the *Couples Only* sign and sat down to play.

Mick skated over to Lisa, who was waiting at the guardrail. He took her hands and crossed both of them together in his. They went onto the floor as Rosemary began to play a soft number.

"Why don't we go to the movies next week?" Lisa asked.

"I don't like the movies. They're boring."

"How about going for a pizza, or a walk, or something—anything?"

"Lisa, I've told you a million times that I don't have time to go out with you. All week long I'm caged in at Foods-For-You. When the weekend comes around, particularly Sunday, which is my one day off, I have a lot to do. Really!"

"You mean you *won't* go out with me."

"Have it your way," he replied.

She remained silent.

Mick liked Lisa as a friend and as a skating partner but he didn't like her enough to date her. It always ended up with small talk and a commitment. He'd rather keep her as a friend—a good friend. Lately she came on too strong for him.

On the third time around he noticed someone he hadn't seen at the rink before—someone who was staring at him. On the next round, he led Lisa close to the guardrail. When he passed, the girl smiled at him. He smiled back.

"Who's she?" Lisa inquired, never missing anything.

"I don't know. Never saw her before. You?"

"No. She's kind of skinny."

When Couples Only ended, Rosemary put back on the brights, changed the card to *All Skate,* and began playing an upbeat number. Mick skated over to where J.P. was sitting.

"See that girl over there? The one in the plaid skirt?"

"Yeah. What about her?"

"Ever see her here before?"

"No."

"I think she's all by herself. Why don't you ask her out on the next Couples Only?"

"Some chance," J.P. said. "She'd only say no. Besides, I can't skate with anyone else. My feet get all tangled. I'd probably topple the two of us over."

"I'm going to ask her then."

"Be my guest."

"See you later," he said, dashing across the rink to where she was sitting.

"Hi," he said.

"Hi," she said back.

"Do you come here often?"

"No. It's my first time."

"I didn't think I saw you here before," he said.

"Do you come here often?" she asked.

"Yeah. I come here quite a lot. Sometimes I think I live here. Can I buy you a Coke?"

"No, thanks."

"Where are you from?"

"From?"

"Yeah—*from*. Where do you live?"

"Montclair."

"You here by yourself?"

"Yes."

"Drive here?"

"No. I don't have a car."

"Come by bus?"

"No. My mother dropped me off."

"How will you get home? Montclair's pretty far, isn't it?"

"The answer to your first question is my mother's picking me up at ten o'clock. The answer to your second question is yes."

"How long a drive?"

"About forty minutes by car."

"You're right. It's far. Sure you don't want a Coke?"

"Positive."

He didn't know what else to say. He stood looking at her, her at him. Neither said a word.

Breaking the silence, Mick again asked, "Are you sure you don't want a Coke?"

"You asked me that three times. Twice I said no.

Now I'm saying no for the third time. You ask a lot of questions."

"I'm sorry. I don't mean to. I just thought I'd like to meet you. My name's Mick—Mick Thompson," he said, awkwardly extending his hand to hers.

"I'm Kitty," she said, taking his hand. "Kitty Rhoades."

After a few seconds she broke the silence again, asking, "Can I have it back?"

"What?" he asked.

"My hand. You're holding my hand."

"I'm sorry."

"That's O.K."

"Hey, would you like to skate on the next Couples Only?"

"I've got to warn you that I'm not too good. I've only been skating a couple of years on and off— mostly off. I used to go to Glider's Rink in Montclair before they closed it last spring. I watched you skate tonight. I saw you do the last Couples Only."

"I know. We smiled at each other, didn't we? That's why I came over to say hello."

Kitty was embarrassed. "I didn't really smile *at* you. I smiled because you were skating so well. The girl you skated with is good, too."

"Lisa," Mick said, bending down to tighten a lace.

"Kitty."

"What?"

"Kitty. My name is Kitty."

48

"No, I mean Lisa is the girl I skated with. She is good. What about the next Couples Only? You didn't answer me."

"O.K., I'll give it a try. If you don't like the way I skate, you can tell me and we can get off the floor."

"You'll be fine. You can't be that bad."

Rosemary clicked the microphone, testing it to see if it was on.

"Ro's going to talk. It's near time for the first Trio."

"Who's Ro?"

"She's Ro," he said, pointing up to her, "the organist. Her name's Rosemary, but everyone calls her Ro."

"Oh."

"She always does her welcome bit before the first Trio."

"Boys and girls, men and women, and anything else here tonight on wheels, on behalf of our entire staff I'd like to welcome you once again to Wonder Wheels—Home of the Best. If you've been here before, welcome back. If you're here for the first time, come back well. My name is Rosemary—Rosemary Wilson, your organist. If you've any special requests, just let me know—musical requests that is! There's no charge and no tipping allowed—unfortunately," she added with a small affected laugh, loudly playing the first eight notes of Beethoven's "Fifth Symphony"—*Da-Da-Da-Da, Da-Da-Da-Da.*

"She's funny," Kitty said.

"She's great," Mick answered. "I love her."

"And now it's time for a brief three-minute record break," Rosemary continued. "Even your loyal organist has to go to the john once in a while. So skate to the music of Papa Bandana's band, and when I return, which *will* be promptly, Wonder Wheels will have it's first Trio of the evening. Get your partners together and let's see a good show out there. Once again, this is Rosemary—Rosemary Wilson—*your* organist, warmly welcoming you to Wonder Wheels."

"I promised I'd skate on the first Trio with two of my friends," Mick said. "I'm meeting them at the Coke machine. Want to meet them?"

"Not right now. I think I'll just skate around the outside of the rink for a while. I'll practice for our Couples Only."

"O.K. I'll meet you here after the number, O.K.?"

"Fine."

"See you later, Kitty," Mick said, skating away.

Kitty watched him glide, then stop short on his skates, turn around, and skate back to her. "I promise I won't ask too many questions," he said.

She smiled.

He went off again.

She watched him again.

.   .   .

"Where's Lisa?" Mick asked Jingo who was already waiting.

"She's in the ladies' room. She'll be out in a minute."

"I see you met her," J.P. said, licking on a chocolate ice cream bar.

"Her name's Kitty. She's new here. Her first time."

"Where is she?" Jingo asked.

"Over there," he pointed.

"Why don't you introduce us?" Jingo asked.

"I asked her to come over but she didn't want to."

"Her loss," said Jingo.

Mary Lou rolled out of the ladies' room.

"Lisa still in there?" Jingo asked.

"She'll be right out. She's talking with Ro."

"What do you do in that place? It's like a meeting hall."

"I'll never tell," Mary Lou answered. "So you'll never ever find out. Is my gorgeous *Poo-air toe-ree-can* going to tear up the rink on the Trio?" she asked, petting Jingo's hair.

"Cool it, girl. I just combed. Save it for later at Pop's Pizza."

Rosemary and Lisa came out of the ladies' room together.

"I thought you fell in," Jingo said to Lisa.

"Why do you always say that? You know what? You're coarse."

"Coarse? Listen to the lady's cool word. Coarse!

If you wanna see something coarse, I can show it to you," he said, grabbing his groin.

"Coarse!" Lisa snapped again.

"Cool it, my lovelies," Rosemary said. "Save the energy for your wheels."

"What are you playing, Ro?" Mick asked.

"How 'bout 'People'?"

"Yuck!" J.P. uttered between licks.

"What's the matter with you?" Rosemary asked, dramatically raising her left eyebrow. "You don't like the way I play 'People'?"

"Play anything but 'People'," J.P. said. "Anything!"

"Maybe you'd like 'The Star-Spangled Banner'? Ah, I remember playing that the night of September 14, 1814, for Frances Scott Key, when the bombs were bursting in mid-air. Now there was a man!"

The group roared.

"To make you happy—since it's Rosemary's policy to always want to make everybody happy—especially Wonder Wheels regulars—how's 'When the Saints Come Marching In'?"

"Great," J.P. said. "Anything but 'People,' please?"

Rosemary walked away smiling.

"Come on, J.P.," Mary Lou said, "let's go sit and watch."

Mick, Lisa, and Jingo skated over to an entrance waiting for Rosemary to put on the Trio sign. She clicked the microphone again.

"Ladies and whatever," she began. "I have a special request from one of our Wonder Wheel regulars. Remember, you don't have to be a regular to request a song. Just let Rosemary know what you'd like to hear and I'll tinkle it out on my dainty fingers for your delight and pleasure. For tonight's first Trio, I'm playing a special request from J.P. Johnson. The song," she said, pausing and looking straight down at J.P., "is 'People.'"

J.P. clapped his hands over his ears. Mary Lou roared. Mick, Lisa, and Jingo did, too.

"That'll teach ice-cream lips to open his mouth on Ro," Jingo said. "She's great. Come on. Let's fly."

The floor was crowded with threesomes. Mick, Lisa, and Jingo stayed in the center, where only the better skaters rolled.

"This is too slow to fly to," Jingo said.

"I feel like we're standing still," Lisa added. "I could kill J.P. What's the matter with Ro? 'People' is a good Couples number. It doesn't work for Trios."

"Ro'll upbeat it soon," Mick said.

"Let's tell her to," said Jingo, leading them from the center of the rink closer to the organ.

"Give us a break, Ro," Jingo called up to her.

She winked at him. Finishing 'People,' she immediately went into 'When the Saints Come Marching In.'

"That's better," Lisa said.

"Ready, Mick?" Jingo asked.

"Ready."

"Let's fly."

They went back to the center of the rink and slowly started a Peabody, a fast-traveling dance demanding agility and a lot of space, a dance that allowed them to move as one both horizontally and vertically.

Several threesomes moved away to give them room. Others stopped and stood against the inside of the guardrail to watch.

They looked like graceful seagulls, skating as if they were on air rather than on wheels.

"Ready to bend?" Mick asked Jingo.

"Top of the next bar," Jingo answered.

At once the three stretched out their arms horizontally. As Rosemary played faster they gained speed, then, bending their knees down almost touching the floor, they skated, coming back up in unison, going down again, and while down moving closer together, skating in the position for as long as they could hold it. Coming up, they formed a circle and began spinning. Everyone's eyes were on them.

They spun for the rest of the song, ending on a dead halt at the last note.

Everyone applauded.

Rosemary put the *All Skate* card back, and the rink became jammed again.

"Whew!" Lisa exclaimed. "That was fantastic."

"You were good, Lisa," Mick said.

"Do it again later?" asked Jingo.

"Why not?" Mick answered. "When I get going like that I could skate forever."

"I'm going to rest," Jingo said. "See you both later."

"Me, too," Lisa said. "I'm soaked. Want to do the next Couples, Mick?"

"I'm promised."

"You skating with Mary Lou?"

"No."

"Who?"

"Skinny," Mick answered.

"Who?"

"The girl you said looked skinny."

"How about the last one?"

"You're on. See you later, Lisa."

Mick looked around the rink for Kitty. Couples Only had already begun.

"Here I am," she said, skating toward him. "I was reading the bulletin board and forgot. I'm sorry."

"Ready?" he asked.

"You must be kidding," she answered. "I saw you do that Trio. You're fantastic."

"Come on," he said, putting his hands around her waist and leading her onto the floor. "You're not so bad," he added as they began to roll.

"Next to you, I'm the pits."

"Loosen up a little. You're too tight."

"If I loosen up, I'll go right on my face and take you with me."

"No chance," he said. "Just try to loosen up a bit. Think feet. You won't fall when I'm holding you."

Feet were the last thing Kitty could think of. She concentrated on each and every movement. In between she thought how good it was to be skating with him. He held her strongly. She liked the way she felt with him.

"Kitty?" Mick asked.

"Yes?"

"No. I mean Kitty. Your name is Kitty."

"You just won the $164,000 question. Yes, me Kitty, you Mick."

He smiled but didn't say another word. He liked the way she felt with him, too.

6

KITTY HAD ONLY MET MICK a few times at Wonder Wheels. She had liked him right away, and more each time they were together. She was thinking about him when the telephone rang. She jumped up from the dinner table. "I'll get it," she said.

"Sit down," her mother said sternly. "Let it ring five times."

"I'm positive it's for me, Mom. I'm expecting a call."

"I *said* sit down. I'll answer it when it rings once more. You know the telephone rules in this house— five rings before you pick up the phone."

After the fifth ring, Mrs. Rhoades answered the telephone. "Hello?" she asked.

"Hi. Is Kitty there, please?"

"Who's calling?"

"This is Mick. Mick Thompson."

"Kitty is just finishing her dinner. Call back in about fifteen minutes. She'll be able to talk with you then," she said and hung up.

"Was that Mick?" Kitty asked, both frustrated and disgusted, knowing it was him.

"Yes. Finish your dinner."

"I am finished. Mother, that was mean of you. I could have taken that call. I told you I was expecting a call."

"Don't you *ever* tell me I'm mean, do you hear? Who do you think you are? If it's important, he'll call back."

"Was that for me, Doris?" Grandma Perkins called from the bedroom.

"No, Mama. It was for Kitty."

"You sure it wasn't for me? You sure? I think Daddy's going to call me tonight. Are you sure it wasn't Daddy?"

"No, Mama. I told you it was for Kitty."

"Kitty, Kitty, Kitty! Every time the phone rings it's for Kitty. Tell her not to talk too long. I'm expecting Daddy to call me tonight. Do you hear me, Doris?"

"I hear you, Mama."

"Can I be excused?" Kitty asked.

"No. Sit there! I want to talk with you about—"

Kitty's brother Billy interrupted her with, "Why

58

does she always ask the same old thing every time the phone rings? Ever since I can remember she's asked that dumb question. Why don't you just tell her that Grandpa's dead when she asks that?"

"Shut up! I told you not to ask questions about Grandma's problem. She's old and she just forgets."

"I think she's getting crazier," he said.

"I don't want to hear you talk like that ever again. Go to your room."

He slapped the napkin down on his plate, got up, scowled as if wanting to say something, but held it in and left the kitchen.

"You see that?" she said to Kitty. "You see that temper in his face? Just like your father."

"He didn't mean anything by it," Kitty said.

"Stick up for him. Go ahead. I wish someone would stick up for me sometime. The two of you come and go as you please. If either one of you had even half the responsibility I have, you wouldn't be so flippant. I work day in and day out at that plant to support all of us. And day in and day out I have to put up with Mama. Don't you think I get tired of all this?"

Kitty remained silent. She knew it was no use arguing with her mother. She never could win. Sometimes the tension in the house ran so high that she wanted to scream. She knew how hard her mother's life was, but she couldn't do anything about it.

Kitty's father walked out one night about four years ago and never came back. For two years her mother tried desperately to find out where he was. No one could trace him. He just vanished.

Billy was only eight years old when he left and missed him terribly. For months on end he cried and cried at night, wanting his father to come home.

Kitty didn't. The only thoughts she had of her father were unkind ones, thoughts of his screaming at her mother, her screaming back, constant fighting and arguing, bickering over nothing. Her mother was just as bad. She seemed to find something to fight about even when there wasn't anything wrong.

After Kitty's father left, her mother was forced to get a job to make ends meet. And a year after her father left, her grandfather died, which further complicated everyone's life because Grandma Perkins came to live with them.

It wasn't so bad in the beginning. Grandma Perkins was able to help with the household chores; she cooked, cleaned, sewed, and looked after Kitty and Billy while their mother worked. That only lasted for a few months, however. Grandma Perkins had a stroke, which caused her mind to go off into fantasies about her late husband. There was nothing to do but be patient with her.

"Doris!" Grandma Perkins called.

"Yes, Mama," Mrs. Rhoades answered.

"I want my pills and some water now. Bring them in to me, Doris. *Now.*"

"Yes, Mama," she answered. "Billy!" she called.

"What?" he asked in an angry tone.

"Come in here and get Grandma's pills."

Still scowling, Billy walked back into the kitchen. "Where are they?" he asked.

"The same place they always are. On the shelf in the box."

He went to the cupboard and took two candy hearts from a box marked *Dear Hearts—100% Pure Sugar—A Product Made in U.S.A.* Smiling, he said, "How's these? I'll give her one Cool and one Turned On."

"Don't be smart," his mother said. "Just bring them to her with a glass of water."

He poured a glass of water and took it, along with the candy, to his grandmother's room.

"Now who is this kid who called?"

"He's a guy I met at the skating rink."

"Is that the reason why all of a sudden you're traipsing into Newark so frequently? How old is he?"

"About my age, I guess."

"Don't you even know how old he is? Have you seen him outside the rink?"

"No, Mother. I meet him there. There're a lot of kids my age who go skating."

"I don't care about other kids. Why is he calling you?"

"He probably just wants to know if I'll be at the rink tomorrow night, that's all."

"That better be *all!* I don't like you running around with strange boys. I don't know why you won't go steady with Kenneth. He's a good person. There's a future for the two of you if you'd only let it come about. He's friendly, good to his mother, has a responsible job at Macy's, and he goes to church regularly."

Kenneth! The mere mention of his name sent a shiver down Kitty's spine.

"I don't like Kenneth," she said. "He's too old for me."

"Old? Twenty is old by you? What difference does three years make? Your father was twenty-four when I married him. And I was only nineteen. That was five years' difference. In September you'll be a senior in high school. You've got to start thinking about your future. I don't think it's healthy for you to be fooling around with some stranger from a skating rink. Kenneth is mature. He's responsible."

Kitty had had enough. She would have loved to answer back with something like, "Then why don't you go out with him?" Instead she just stared at the kitchen clock, watching the secondhand sweep by, waiting for the big hand to reach the minute when Mick would call back.

"There's something else you should know about Kenneth. Reverend Goodbar's wife told Mrs. Geisner that next year Kenneth just might become a deacon at the church. Do you know what that means? It means history, that's what it means. Kenneth Delaney will become the youngest deacon Mount Sinai Presbyterian Church ever had. Mrs. Delaney is just riding high on the hog over it—proud as proud could be. I want to live to see the day I become proud of something one of you two do. Anything.

"Let's get this mess cleaned up," she added, picking up the dinner plates.

Kitty was relieved that the lecture was over if even for a few minutes. She began clearing the table.

"Doris! Doris!" Grandma Perkins called.

"Yes, Mama?"

"When are you going to bring me my pills? I need them. Now!"

"Billy!" Mrs. Rhoades shrieked.

"What do you want now?" he asked, coming into the kitchen.

"Didn't I tell you to bring Grandma her pills?"

"I *did* bring them to her."

"Bring her another one. Here," she said, reaching into the box, handing him one of the candy hearts.

"She's becoming a one hundred percent sugar freak," he said. "Do you really believe she thinks this is medicine?"

"I don't care *what* she thinks it is. They keep her quiet. Just bring it to her."

"Doris! Doris!" Grandma Perkins called again.

"Coming, Mama. Billy's bringing you your pill."

"Sometimes I think I'm living in a mental institution," Billy said.

His mother didn't answer.

Kitty turned toward the window, biting her lips together to keep from laughing out loud.

Glancing toward the telephone she thought, *Ring phone, ring. Please ring!*

7

"HI, MOM," Mick called as he walked in from work.

"Hi, honey. Have a good day?"

"It was O.K. I was on the register all day. Sometimes it gets so boring I could die. I don't know how someone like Eileen can spend her whole life behind a cash register."

"Someone has to do it."

"I know. But it seems so fruitless—day in, day out, punching keys for an entire lifetime."

"When people have secure jobs they aren't likely to change them quickly, particularly in today's times."

"Quickly? She's been there fifteen years and never missed a single day. Can you believe that?"

"I can believe anything! She probably doesn't know anything else."

"Wouldn't you think she'd try to do something else? Or at least *think* about doing something different?"

"How do you know she doesn't think about doing something else and is afraid to make a change? Besides, she's not a young girl. Jobs are hard to get, and they're particularly hard to get if you're an older woman without skills."

"What would you do? I mean if something happened to Dad?"

"Mick! Don't talk like that."

"Why not? What would you do?"

"Well, for one thing I could back into teaching, God forbid! It's an impossible job today. Or I'd let *you* support me. I'd come to live with you and be a doting grandmother. Now I think that's enough of a conversation that is really going nowhere at all. Let's change the subject please?"

"O.K. What's for supper?"

"Pork chops."

"Great. What time will Dad be home?"

"Regular."

"Great again."

"He's been working long hours this month. It's that time of year again. He's had all kinds of reports to do. But he closed them out last Friday. Oh, there's some mail for you. I put it on your desk."

"Anything important?"

"Just a few catalogs for skate equipment."

66

"How do they get my name? I get more stupid catalogs. If you bought even half the stuff they offered to put on your skates, you'd be so bogged down you wouldn't be able to move your feet."

"Is J.P. taking you to the rink tonight?"

"No. He has to work late at the record shop."

"Dad or I will drive you."

"Thanks, but you don't have to. I'll walk. It's beautiful out. I can use the time to think."

" 'Bout what?"

"The audition, for one thing. It's on my mind."

"I know. But don't worry too much about it. It won't be the end of the world if you don't get that job."

"I know. But everyone seems so sure I'll win. I'd really like to, Mom. I'd like to go away next summer. I know I don't want to do the supermarket routine again."

"Is your friend meeting you again tonight?"

"You mean Kitty? Yeah," he said, smiling, his whole face lighting up.

"You really seem to like her."

"She's nice. I like talking with her."

"Anything serious going on between the two of you? Like something a probing mother should know about?"

"I don't know. I've only seen her a few times at the rink. But I wouldn't mind it if there was. She's really different from the other kids."

"In what way?"

"Well, take Lisa, for example. Sometimes she thinks she knows everything and she's becoming more possessive than ever. And Mary Lou acts like a baby. She's so immature. All she does is coo and hang on Jingo like someone holds a dog on a leash."

"Ah! The problems of young love. Jingo and Mary Lou have been a twosome since sixth grade, haven't they?"

"Yeah, and they get worse every day."

"How is Jingo? He hasn't come around since school ended."

"He's O.K."

"Still tap dancing?"

"Like a demon. He's great on wheels."

"Say hello to him for me. Mary Lou and Lisa, too. Why don't you invite them all over some Sunday afternoon. Kitty, too. I'd enjoy meeting her. Tell me more about her, Mick."

"There's nothing to tell you."

"You just said she's different. How so?"

"She's—she's sensitive. I mean like she's serious about things. She's intelligent, yet shy, and she doesn't mouth off a lot about nothing like most of the kids do."

"She sounds great to me."

"She is, Mom. She really is."

"As much as I'd love to talk with you more, I just

have to start supper. Pork chops don't get baked with conversation. Hey! I really don't want you to worry about the audition. You'll do the best you can. That's all anyone can expect. You're beginning to make me anxious about it. I can't wait."

"Are you and Dad really coming?"

"Are you crazy? We wouldn't miss it for anything."

Mick sat looking back and forth between the clock over the organ and the entrance to the rink. It was nine o'clock and Kitty hadn't come.

"Hi, handsome," Lisa said, skating over to him. "She stood you up, huh?"

"Maybe she missed the bus or something," Mick said.

"Maybe she just stood you up. The first Couples Only is coming up in a few minutes. Do you want to skate with me or just sit here moping over Miss Thing?"

"O.K.," Mick mumbled, his eyes fixed on the entrance.

"Don't sound so excited," Lisa said. "You might just have a heart attack and die right on the spot."

"Cool it, Lisa. Meet me here for the Couples Only. I have to go and find Ange and ask him something."

He skated away to the doorway, hoping he might

see Kitty walk down from the bus station. She was nowhere in sight. He reached into his pocket for some change, went to the pay phone, and dialed her number.

"Hello?" a voice answered.

"Hi, is Kitty there?"

"Uh-uh."

"Who is this?" Mick asked.

"Billy. I'm Kitty's brother."

"Oh, hi. My name is Mick. I'm a friend of Kitty's. She told me about you."

"I know. You're the great skater. Kitty told me about you, too."

Mick smiled and asked, "Do you know where she is?"

"She said she was going to Wonder Wheels."

"Do you know when she left?"

"Uh-uh."

"Can I speak to your mother?"

"Uh-uh. She's next door. The only ones home are me and my grandmother, and you wouldn't want to talk to her."

"O.K. Thanks, Billy. If Kitty does come home, will you tell her I called?"

"Sure."

" 'Bye."

" 'Bye."

"Well," Lisa said as he opened up the pay-phone

door. "You told me to meet you there," she added, pointing toward the bench. "Couples Only has already started, or haven't you noticed? I'm not in the habit of waiting for, or running after, guys to skate with me, you know."

"I'm sorry Lisa. Let's skate. But do me a favor?"

"What?"

"Just shut up."

A few minutes into the number, Mick saw Kitty walk into the rink.

"Let's break," he said to Lisa. "Kitty's here."

"What? In the middle of Couples Only?"

"Come on," he said, leading her to the guardrail.

"Maybe I should ask Ro to play 'All Hail the Queen' for her big entrance."

Mick just shook his head. He skated over to Kitty.

"Hi," he said. "You're late. I was getting worried."

"That's nice," she answered. "No one ever worries about me."

"I even called your house."

"Oh, no! Did my mother answer?"

"No. Billy did. He said your mother was next door or something and he was there with your grandmother.

"Thank God. She would've flipped out. Mick, do me a favor. I think it would be best not to call my house too often, O.K.? If we have to talk, let me call you."

"Why?"

"I'll explain some other time. My mother doesn't like me to get calls."

"How come you're so late? That's the reason I called."

"I missed the bus and had to wait forever for another one. How come you're not skating?"

"I was. I stopped when I saw you come in."

"Thanks. That's nice, too. But why don't you go back in till I change and get my skates on?"

"I'd rather wait for you."

"Hey! That's also nice. You must've taken nice pills tonight."

"No, it's just that—" He stopped before he said what he was thinking.

"Just that what?"

"Nothing."

"I thought you were going to say something like—" She stopped too.

"Like what?" Mick pressed.

"Like I think you know what and I think I know what."

"You're right," Mick laughed. "You're *so* right. Come on, get ready. I want to hold you."

With the exception of the Trios, Mick and Kitty skated together all night. They didn't say much to one another; they didn't have to.

During the last Couples Only, Mick asked, "Are you going to stay to watch me practice?"

"I'd love to, but I can't. It'll be too late. It's a long ride home."

"Damn! I wish I could drive," Mick said.

"I wish you could, too. Buses are boring."

"Kitty?" Mick asked.

"Yes?"

"Nothing."

"You want to ask me something?"

"No. Yes. No."

"Well, make up your mind."

"Will I see you Saturday night?"

"I can't come Saturday night, Mick. I have to go somewhere else."

"Damn again. Can't you get out of it?"

"No. If I could I would, but I can't."

"Then I have to wait until next Wednesday to see you again?"

"What are you doing Sunday?"

"Nothing."

"Me either. Want to do nothing together?"

"Great! What would you like to do?" asked Mick.

"Nothing."

"How do we do nothing?"

"Easy. I'll meet you and we'll just do nothing— together. We'll walk in a park, talk—anything and nothing."

"You're on. Where will I meet you?"

"Meet me at the bus stop in front of the rink. How's two o'clock?"

"How's twelve?"

"Let's compromise. I'll meet you at one."

"How's twelve?" Mick asked again.

"I can't make it that early. I have to go to church. Make it one."

"Fine. One o'clock at the bus stop. I'll look for you."

"Me too."

He held her tighter, skating slowly to the music.

"Mick? I have something to tell you," she said.

"What?"

"I like you very much."

Mick smiled and squeezed her hands. "I like you very much, too," he said. "I really do."

.

8

HE COULDN'T UNDERSTAND THE FEELING but he knew it was there, bothering him on and off—mostly on. Occasionally he'd stare toward the entrance, wishfully thinking that Kitty would walk in. He knew she wouldn't and wondered why the thought came into his head.

Before the last Couples Only, he skated over to the bench where he had first met Kitty. He sat down, placing his left arm over the back of the bench as if he could feel her being there with him. This was the longest and loneliest Saturday night he had ever spent at Wonder Wheels. He missed Kitty. He couldn't wait until tomorrow.

When he was skating with Lisa on the last Couples Only, he said, "Lisa Wells, I'm proud of you."

"What did I do to deserve such a compliment?" Lisa asked.

"You didn't ask one single question about Kitty's not being here tonight, and you didn't even make one of your raunchy remarks about her."

"I knew she wasn't coming tonight. J.P. told me."

"J.P. should publish a Wonder Wheels gossip sheet! You don't like her, do you?" Mick asked.

"I like her but I don't really know her. When she's here she's always with you. When she is with us she doesn't say much. Look, I promised myself *not* to talk with you about Kitty unless you wanted to talk to *me* about her."

"There's nothing to talk about."

"There's a lot to talk about, but it's none of my business."

"What is there to talk about?"

"The main thing is that you're hung up on her."

"So?"

"So I'm jealous, that's all."

"Jealous? What are you jealous about?"

"You really don't understand me, do you Mick? You know how much I care for you—how I've always felt about you. It shouldn't come as a surprise now."

"I *do* understand, Lisa. It's just that—"

"It's just that it's not the way I'd like it to be and I've got to get that through my head once and for all. It's my problem, Mick, not yours. I just thought that this summer would turn out different, that's all."

"How?"

"Between us. I really thought there was something there."

"There is, Lisa, in so many ways."

"Thanks for saying that. But it's not the right ways."

When Couples Only ended, they skated over to the Coke machine.

"Are we all going to meet over at Pop's Pizza tonight?" Jingo asked.

"I can't," Lisa answered. "I asked my dad to pick me up."

"So? Have him join us."

"Are you crazy, Jingo? The last thing in the world my father would like to do is have pizza at eleven o'clock at night with his daughter and her friends. And the last thing in the world I'd like to do is have pizza with my friends while my father sat there juggling and struggling with mozzarella cheese. Count me out."

"Mick?" asked Jingo.

"Not tonight, Jing. Ange is letting me lock up. I've some ideas I want to work out for the new routine. I've been blocking steps out in my head all week—between the clanging of cash registers and customers crying over food prices going up. J.P. is staying with me to work the tape."

"Why didn't you tell me?" Lisa asked. "I could've stayed, too. I could use all the practice I can get."

"I didn't know until about an hour ago, Lisa. You know how Ange is sometimes, especially on Saturday nights. I really didn't know."

"Well, it looks like it's just me and you," Jingo said to Mary Lou, loudly wailing, "*R-r-r-oomph, r-r-r-oomph,*" imitating the starting sound of his car's engine.

"Sometimes you're so-o-o-o bad, Jingo," Mary Lou said, "but that's why I love you so."

Within the next half hour the rink began emptying, once again taking on its unique characteristic of stillness.

"I'll go out to the car and get the recorder," J.P. told Mick. "Be right back."

"Closing up tonight, Mick?" asked Rosemary.

"Yeah, Ange is letting me stay."

"You know, Tiger, if you want me to stay to play for you some night I'd be glad to. Not tonight, though. I'm bushed! The old gal ain't what she used to be."

"Thanks, Ro, but I think it's better for me to practice with a recording. I've got to use it for the audition anyway."

"That's good thinking. Besides, who in the hell wants to hear organ music anymore, except at a church or a funeral parlor. If it weren't for Ange

78

I'd be tinkling the keys in some piano-bar some-where until the wee hours of the morning, playing for people who don't want to listen anyway. Few rinks have live music anymore, if you can call *me* alive. Everything's canned and overloud. In twenty years or less everyone is going to go deaf. If you were smart you'd become an ear doctor. There's where the real bread's going to be. Mark my words.

"Whoo! I never remember being so tired. Oh, by the way, I have something personal to tell you, kid —before the audition."

"What's that, Ro?" Mick asked.

"It can wait a spell if you're not in the mood for criticism."

"I'm in the mood for criticism from you anytime. Is there something wrong with my skating?"

"No, your skating's greater than ever."

"Well, what is it? Is it about Kitty?"

"No, it has nothing to do with Kitty. I like her cool style. She's a nice kid. What I wanted to tell you was to change your underwear."

"What?" Mick asked, totally unprepared for the remark, breaking up with laughter.

"Change your underwear—your shorts. They sag. I can see them sagging through your pants. They'll look even worse under your costume. Get something that fits. Invest a few bucks on jockey shorts. Boxers are for kids and older men who don't have anything to show off. You, of all specimens of manhood, don't need them. Now I've said my piece, so good night."

"Good night, Ro. Thanks for the advice. I never thought about my shorts," he said, smiling.

"You know I don't give out much criticism, particularly to you, but I had to tell you. Here's a kiss for luck for tonight's practice session," she added, giving him a fond peck on his cheek.

" 'Bye, Ro. Thanks again."

"Remember me in your will. Ta-ta, Tiger," she said, leaving the rink.

9

KITTY LOOKED AT HER WATCH. It was four fifteen.
Then she looked at Mick lying fast asleep in her
arms. He began feeling heavier on her slim body,
but she didn't want to move him for fear she'd
disturb his nap.

It was hot—very hot. She was glad they'd settled
under a huge old tree; the strong, wide trunk gave
support to her back and the leafy branches let in
an occasional summer breeze.

Now and then she tenderly wiped some beads of
sweat from his forehead and fanned his face with
her handkerchief to try to keep him cooler. He was
sleeping as soundly as a newborn baby.

The three hours they had been together had
darted by like three seconds. With Mick, everything
unpleasant in her life seemed to disappear—the
anger and frustration of her mother, her grand-

mother's peculiarities, and especially her horrid relationship with Kenneth, one foisted upon and fos-
tered by her mother.

In three hours she had learned more about Mick
than she ever could have learned from being with
him at Wonder Wheels. He had talked endlessly
about his family, about his job at Foods-For-You,
about his ambition to win the upcoming audition
so that he could spend next summer doing what he
really wanted to do.

It was the first time she had opened up with him,
too. It wasn't as if she'd wanted to hold anything
back, but time had never really allowed her to discuss her family situation before.

He began to stir. She looked at him, studying his
strong facial features—his arms, hands, and long
muscular legs that seemed to stretch out forever.

The one thing she felt guilty about was not men-
tioning Kenneth to him. She knew he'd understand
the situation, but didn't feel she wanted to waste a
single second of their time together talking about
him, especially since she was going to put a stop to
that relationship the minute she could.

She also didn't want Mick to feel that it was because they had met that she was ending a relationship with Kenneth. Long before she had met Mick
at Wonder Wheels, Kenneth had been a thorn in
her side.

She had met Kenneth at a church picnic last summer. He seemed pleasant, and since both their mothers were on the same committee, their paths crossed frequently—but always when other people were around.

Several months after they had met, Kenneth asked her mother's permission to take her to a movie. Her mother was impressed with his asking and with the fact that he was a regular parishioner.

Kenneth seemed to be loving and caring—traits that attracted Kitty to him. Kenneth was all right as long as she didn't mention anyone else to him. The minute she did, he became aggressive, insisting she was "his"—that she couldn't go out with anybody else.

At first Kitty thought he was just kidding, but incident after incident proved that he really believed she belonged to him. It was as if he owned her, the way someone owns a pet.

As much as she tried, there was no way she could reach him. He was so adamant on the point that she began to be afraid of him.

The worst incident had occurred in May. She had accepted an invitation to go to the end-of-the-year school dance with Jason Potter. When she told Kenneth about it, he twisted her arm around her back, threatening to break it off if she didn't cancel the date. She knew then that she was in a predicament —Kenneth was sick. She broke the date with Jason, hating herself for doing it.

After the incident she avoided Kenneth as much as she could, but he kept popping up in her life like a nightmare. Several times she tried to discuss the situation with her mother, but she wouldn't listen. She was hung up on Kenneth. She kept reminding Kitty of his maturity, his responsible ways, his dedication to the church.

The very thought of Kenneth made Kitty feel sick. She would tell Mick about him—when she could. At the right time, in the right place, at the right moment, preferably after she had ended it once and for all with Kenneth. The whole ridiculous encounter would only be a memory.

"I've got to get the right music, J.P. Got to!" Mick mumbled in his sleep.

"You'll find it," Kitty whispered, stroking Mick's hair. "Sh-h-h!"

"What? Oh, man! Damn! What time is it?" he asked, opening his eyes, quickly closing them again to block out the shining light of the sun.

"Four thirty," Kitty said. "You dozed off."

"Why did you let me? Why didn't you wake me?"

"I let you 'cause you did, and I didn't 'cause I didn't want to."

"I'm sorry, Kitty."

"There's nothing to be sorry about. You only napped for about twenty minutes."

"Seems like twenty years. I feel like Rip Van Winkle. Hot, isn't it?"

"Terrible, but lying under this tree feels good. At least there's a little whoosh of breeze now and then."

"It was stupid of me to fall asleep."

"It wasn't stupid. You must've been tired."

"I never fall asleep in the middle of the afternoon like that. Never. The last thing I remember talking to you about was practicing the routine last night, then nothing until now, except I knew you were here. I knew I was with you."

"No you didn't. You were with J.P."

"What?"

"You were thinking about J.P. Just before you woke up you were actually talking in your sleep about J.P. finding the right music for your routine."

"My subconscious might have been with J.P. wondering about the music. My body knew it was with you."

Kitty smiled. "I knew it was too," she said. "You were getting heavy. Look at my slacks. I'm all wrinkled."

"I'm sorry," Mick replied.

"Stop being sorry. I never met anyone who was sorrier about things that don't make a bit of difference than you."

"Want to go for a walk?" he asked.

"That's a good idea," she answered. "If I sit in this position for even another second, I'm going to sprout roots!"

He extended his hand to help her off the ground. "Want to walk anywhere special?"

"No, let's just walk. It's getting sort of late, Mick, and I have to catch the five twenty-seven bus home. I promised my mother I'd be home for dinner."

"Why don't you call her and tell her you're having dinner at my house, that you'll be home later?"

"But I'm not having dinner at your house."

"You can. My mother would love it. She's dying to meet you. So is my dad. You'll really like them, Kitty."

"As much as I'd like to, Mick, we'll have to make it another time. I don't want to get involved in a million foolish explanations. Since I told her I'd be home for dinner, I'd better stick to it. Let's make it another time, O.K.? I did promise I'd be home."

"I understand. I don't like it, but I understand. Hey, I have an idea. Let's walk down to the supermarket. I'll show you where I work. It's in the same direction as the bus stop anyway."

"Fine," she said, trying to rub the wrinkles from her slacks. "Let's go shopping."

"Shopping? I said we'd walk down to the supermarket. I didn't say anything about shopping. We can look through the window."

"I thought since we're going there we could at least go in. I'd like to see the inside of the store instead of just looking through the window."

"I'm sure you've seen supermarkets before. They're all the same."

"Wrong! The one you work in is different; it's special *because* you work there."

Mick laughed. "Foods-For-You, thank God, is closed on Sundays. If it wasn't, I'd probably be working today. Part-time help gets all the dreg jobs at all the dreg hours. I'm at the point where I can't wait for school to open."

"I felt the same way last summer when I worked in a dress shop. I hated it!"

"Is that why you're not working there this summer?"

"No. My mother figured out that after they deducted everything from my weekly pay, I made less than it cost her to pay a neighbor to take care of my grandmother. So, this summer I'm grandmother-sitting. It's so boring being in the house all day. If Billy wasn't around I'd die of boredom—literally."

"How old is he?"

"Twelve going on forty. He's a great kid. I love him to pieces. If he wasn't around I sometimes think I would have become a runaway."

"That's a pretty strong remark. Things can't be that bad, or can they be?"

"Not really. I learned how to cope when my father left us. I had to. Billy gives me something to live for. Even though he's only twelve, he understands me more than anyone else in the world."

"Till now," Mick said.

"That's nice," Kitty answered.

They walked hand in hand out of the park and down several streets to the small shopping mall where Foods-For-You was located. When they got to the store, Mick pointed out the few places that could be seen from outside, giving her a running commentary on Murph's Throne, the time clock, the other registers, and the express lane.

"See the register marked number two, Kitty? That's where I usually am when I'm not on the floor. It's kind of funny looking from the outside in. Like an empty stage set. I bet it's quieter in there now than it's ever been. You know, all of a sudden I feel stupid."

"Why?" Kitty asked, puzzled over his changing tone and mood.

"Like why did I bring you here? Why in the world would you possibly care to be looking in a supermarket window. I must be going bats!"

"Not at all. It's fun."

"Fun? If this is your idea of fun, next time we're together I'll take you to my closed and empty school. Let's see, the time after that I'll show you the closed and empty bank where I cash my checks. And then—"

"Cut it out. You've made your point. I don't really care what we do as long as we do it together."

"Want to have a soda or something?"

"No, I think we'd better head back toward the bus stop. I can't miss the five twenty-seven. Buses don't run often on Sundays."

As they waited for the bus to come, Mick gazed over at Wonder Wheels. "Looks funny all closed up, doesn't it? It's hard to believe there were hundreds of people there just a few hours ago rolling and rolling around."

"I missed not seeing you skate last night," Kitty said.

"You missed not seeing me skate?"

"Yes, I did. I really did."

"You didn't miss skating *with* me—or miss *me*, the person, Mick Thompson?"

"Don't be silly. Of course I missed you."

"What time is it Kitty?"

"Five thirty," she said, looking at her watch. "The bus is late. It should be here any minute."

"I wish we could turn the clock back to one o'clock. The afternoon flew by, didn't it? I wish you were coming off the bus instead of getting on it."

"Me too."

"I guess I'll see you Wednesday night at Wonder Wheels?"

"Definitely. Wild horses couldn't keep me away."

"Three days and three hours. How can I live without you for so long? Do you think you can stay late on Wednesday to see what I've done so far with my routine? It's really starting to come along the way I want it to."

"I'll try, Mick. But I can't promise. It all depends on the stupid bus schedule. It seems my whole life these days depends on Port Authority."

"Port Authority is coming right now at this very minute," he said looking up the street.

"Yes, that's it all right," Kitty said.

The bus pulled to the corner. Mick took her hand and kissed it. "See you Wednesday, my lady."

"I can't wait. I really can't."

As she boarded the bus, the sudden blast of air-conditioning made her shiver. She took a seat near the window and waved good-bye to Mick.

The bus pulled out. She blew Mick a kiss through the steamed-up window pane.

He blew one back.

10

CANNED CORN WAS THIS WEEK'S SPECIAL at Foods-For-You. The sign on the huge floor display read:
Mix 'em or Match 'em—4 Cans for $1—
With Newspaper Coupon ONLY.

Mick never saw so many cartons of canned corn. Piled downstairs in the stockroom was case after case of creamed corn, whole kernel corn, tender baby kernels packed in water, corn with red-pepper pieces, and corn with mushroom bits.

"Do you really think they'll sell all this corn in one week?" Mick asked Carmen as they piled up the dolly.

"It's a coup special, isn't it? We can sell anything on a coup special. Just watch it disappear. By Saturday morning Murph will be giving out rainchecks for it. Just watch. We'll sell more of this crap in a week with the coups than we'd sell in a month without them. People buy anything that's on sale. It's an old Foods-For-You fact: if something *doesn't* move, put it on sale with a coup and watch it soar. There! That'll do it," Carmen added, placing a last carton on the now-full dolly. "Take this upstairs and start displaying, O.K.?"

"Right on," Mick answered. "I'll come back down for more as soon as I'm finished."

"You don't have to. I'll take over from here. You'd better get going with the p.c.'s or Murph will murder the two of us."

As Mick was stacking the cans of corn, his mind wandered back to Kitty and yesterday. Lately, he found he was thinking of Kitty more and more. Before he met her, all he had on his mind was the upcoming audition. The audition was still on his mind, but thoughts of Kitty stood out over everything else. He thought about her life at home with her mother; about the responsibility of caring for a sickly, senile grandmother; about the strong feelings she had for Billy. He was glad Billy existed. He seemed to be the only person in Kitty's life who gave her some pleasure.

"That's a great job," Carmen said, interrupting his thoughts. "The Jolly Green Giant would be proud of you."

"Want me to help with the rest?" Mick asked.

"No, I'll do it. But you can do me a big favor. This promotion piece has to be dangled from the ceiling. You can reach it easier than I can. Use the step stool."

Mick climbed the three-stepped stool. Carmen handed him an enormous advertisement featuring a blown-up replica of a can of whole kernel corn.

After Mick attached it to the display wire, and was about to step back down, he said, "I must be seeing things! I can't believe it!"

"Believe it," Carmen answered. "You're not seeing things. There's a lot of corn there."

"It's not the corn. It's—forget it." He looked again. He wasn't seeing things. He had to believe it.

He got off the step stool and told Carmen he'd be right back. He dashed down the canned vegetable aisle and raced toward the spaghetti section.

"Kitty!" he exclaimed.

Nonchalantly, as if this was an everyday occurrence, she gave him a quick, "Hi, Mick."

"What are you doing here? Why are you here? How did you get here? I'm flabbergasted!"

"You look it," she said, laughing. "You should see the expression on your face. Oh, I wish I had a camera."

"I *never* would have expected this," he said, still bedazzled at her being there. "How come? Why?"

"Whoa! Before you start one of your royal inquisitions, let me fill you in with some answers. Number one, I came here to see you; number two, I took the bus down here, naturally; and number three, I wanted to surprise you."

"You did!" he said smiling. "Nothing could've surprised me more. But why? Why today?"

"I missed you last night, and I just couldn't wait until next Wednesday to see you."

"It's incredible! You're incredible!" Mick exclaimed. "How did you manage to get a day away from the house and your grandmother?"

"I told my mother I wanted a day off from grandmother-sitting. I told her I wanted to go shopping in Newark and that I was meeting you to go to a movie later."

"What did she say? I mean, yesterday you gave me the bit about her not wanting you to see anyone she hasn't met."

"She said the same thing she always says, 'Nag-gedy-nag-nag-nag. Blah, blah, blah, blah, blah.'"

"She has some vocabulary! Seriously, didn't she mind?"

"I told her I'd invite you up soon and that I really wanted to see you today."

"What about your grandmother?"

"Billy's with her. If he runs into problems there's a neighbor upstairs he can call. She'll be all right. She's stronger than all of us, believe me."

"Right now I'd believe anything. Absolutely anything. But why did you come this early? I don't get off from work until six. It's only twelve thirty."

"Have lunch yet?"

"No, I get my lunch break at one—forty-five measly minutes."

"So? We'll have forty-five measly minutes together. That's better than not seeing you at all, isn't it?"

"You came all the way here from Montclair to see me for forty-five minutes?"

"Yep."

"You're crazy."

"I know. But being crazy with you is fun. If it's O.K. with you, I'll wait around until six when you get off."

"That's four hours' worth of waiting."

"So? I waited all my life to meet you. What's a piddly four hours? After lunch I'll go back to the park and read. The time will pass fast."

"What time do you have to be home?"

"About nine. I can catch the eight o'clock bus."

"Dinner! What about dinner?" he asked, still completely flustered. "Want to come home with me for dinner?"

"Would your parents mind?"

"No, of course not. On Monday nights Dad barbecues. I'll call my mom and have her set out an extra paper plate. She'll be surprised, but not half as surprised as I am. Look, I've got to do some work before lunch. Stay with me. I have to p.c. some pudding."

"P.c.?"

"Price-change. It's a regular routine here. Rub off the old and stick on the new."

"Can I help?"

"No. As a matter of fact, if anyone comes by, make believe you're shopping or something. My boss Murph would have a fit if she knew about this."

"She the heavy-looking woman with glasses sitting atop the Throne?"

"How did you know about the Throne?"

"You told me about her—and it—yesterday, remember?"

"I can't remember anything. I'm in a daze. You've boggled my mind."

"You look so cute in that hat and apron."

"I feel like a fool in it, now more than ever," he said, removing the hat and briskly shaking his head to loosen his hair. "It's my Foods-For-You costume," he added, taking a low, sweeping bow.

"I like it. I'd like you in anything. Hey, I wonder if anyone ever told someone something—something important—in the spaghetti section of a supermarket before."

"What's that?"

"I love you, Mick Thompson. That's why I'm here."

"I love you, too, Kitty," he said. "You're wonderful."

She looked around. "I never felt spaghetti throb before! You'd better get to your pudding."

"Mick," Jessica called. "Angelo's on the phone. He wants to talk with you."

"Excuse me, Kitty," he said.

"Mick, ask Mom to bring out some more ice when she comes, please?"

"Right, Dad."

"Can I get you something else, Kitty?" Jessica asked, coming back onto the deck.

"No, thank you, Mrs. Thompson. I've had more than enough. I really hope this wasn't any trouble for you."

"Don't be silly. I'm glad we had the chance to meet one another. Mick's been talking about you since you met at Wonder Wheels. Will you be going to the audition next month?"

"I wouldn't miss seeing Mick win."

"He's good, isn't he?"

"Fantastic. I've never seen anyone move like he does."

"Are you sure you won't let me drive you home, Kitty?" David asked.

"Positive. I seem to live on buses these days. Besides, it's a long trip to Montclair and back."

"I really wouldn't mind. Mick will keep me company on the way back."

"No, really, Mr. Thompson. I don't mind the bus."

"What did he want, dear?" Jessica asked as Mick came back out.

"It was nothing important. He asked if I'd help out on Wednesday night at the box office. Mrs. Schulman has to take her son somewhere and might be late."

"It's so quiet here," Kitty said.

"Mick! *Mick!* Where are you?"

"It *was* quiet," Mick said. "That's J.P. He usually screams like that."

"MICK!"

"Out here, J.P. In the yard. Stop yelling."

He dashed through the screen door as if the world had just collapsed. He was all out of breath.

"Mick, I found it. Look!" he said, waving an album frantically back and forth. "I've got it. I found it. It's perfect."

"The song? You found the song?" Mick asked, getting up from his chair.

"It came in today. Just a few hours ago. Hi, Mrs. Thompson, Mr. Thompson," he interjected. Then, noticing Kitty, he uttered an enthusiastic, "Hi, Kitty," surprised that she was there.

"Hi, J.P."

Mick took the album from him.

"I was sitting in the sound booth listening to this thing. Side one is the pits. So are the first two bands of side two. I was ready to give up on it when band three comes on. Here, look. It's 'Calliope Girl.' It's unbelievably perfect. Like it was written and arranged just for you. It's by a brand new group, Sons of Fire. It's bound to be a big hit."

"Is it really good?"

"What kind of a question is that? Would I be as excited over this if it wasn't? I couldn't wait to get over here. Let's go in and play it."

"Well, we might as well all go in and listen to it, if it's that good," David said. "Let's go."

J.P. carefully wiped the record, set it on the turntable, and turned it on. Halfway through the song, he asked, "Well, isn't it you? Isn't it all your moves put together? It's like—"

"J.P., please be quiet. Let me hear the rest of it."

It was hard for J.P. to be quiet, but he tried. The second the song ended, he asked, "Well?"

"It's pretty good," David said.

"Catchy tune," Jessica added. "I love the sound of the calliope."

"Kitty?" Mick asked.

"It is you. It's perfect."

"What do *you* think, Mick?" J.P. asked, nearly bursting.

"*Yip-eeee!*" he shouted, standing up and making a double turn as if he were on his skates. Grabbing J.P. and hugging him hard, he said, "J.P., you did it! I knew you would."

"Oh, man. I'm glad you like it."

"The turning/spinning repetition is fantastic. So's the lead in and the bridge and the end."

"I told you, didn't I? It's like they arranged it just for your routine."

"Four stars to Sons of Fire," Mick said.

"Want to hear it again?"

"I want to hear it again *and* again, but not right now. It's near time for your bus, Kitty. We'd better start moving."

"I'll drive you to the bus stop," J.P. said.

"Thanks, J.P., but Kitty and I want to walk."

"Why walk when you can roll?"

"J.P., why don't you stay with us until Mick gets back?" David asked.

"Hey, that's a good idea," Mick said. "When I get back we can listen to the record over and over. You can help me block out some moves."

"Besides," Jessica said, "I have some fresh strawberries. I'll make you some strawberry shortcake."

"Man! How could I refuse that, Mrs. Thompson!" J.P. exclaimed.

"Ready, Kitty?"

"Ready. 'Bye, Mrs. Thompson, Mr. Thompson. Thank you very much for dinner."

"You're quite welcome, Kitty. Come again soon," Jessica said.

"Anytime," David added. " 'Bye, Kitty. It was good meeting you."

"You, too, Mr. Thompson. Thanks again for everything."

" 'Bye, Kitty," said J.P. "Be at Wonder Wheels Wednesday night?"

"I sure will."

"See you then."

"I won't be long. Save a strawberry or two for me," Mick said, leaving the house with Kitty.

"J.P. looked surprised to see me."

"I know. But don't forget I was surprised to see you turn up today, too. You really like the song?"

"I said I did. I really think it's perfect."

"I do, too, but I wanted your stamp of approval."

"You've got it. Consider it one hundred percent stamped."

"How do you like my mom and dad?"

"Consider them one hundred percent stamped, too. Your father is very handsome. And your mom is beautiful. I see where you get your looks from. You all seem so happy together."

"We are happy," he said, wishing he hadn't, remembering how Kitty's home life was totally different from his.

"I'm happy, too, Mick. Happier than I've ever been. I can't wait until Wednesday."

The bus came. Kitty went. As always when she

left, Mick had an empty feeling inside. He stood watching the bus until it was well out of sight. He looked over at Wonder Wheels. If he had the keys he would have opened up and skated all night long.

He began walking home but felt as if he were floating on air. In his mind he was skating, moving to the rhythm of "Calliope Girl," thinking of the audition and J.P. and his mother and father—and Kitty.

11

STARING OUT THE BUS WINDOW, Kitty was thinking about Mick, too. She was glad he had been happy about her showing up at the supermarket. How well the day had turned out. She enjoyed meeting his family, seeing them together. She also thought about what her own life might be like under different circumstances.

"Church Street," the driver called, interrupting her thoughts. "This stop is Church Street. Next stop, Newport Road."

It was only about a five-minute ride from Church Street to Newport Road, Kitty's stop. She continued gazing out the window. Riding by a supermarket, she smiled, thinking about the surprised look on Mick's face when he saw her in the spaghetti section. She'd always remember that.

"Newport," the driver called.

Kitty got up and walked down the aisle, waiting near the front door for the bus to stop. As it pulled into the curb she saw an unwelcome sight. Kenneth was standing at the bus stop. He was the last person on earth she wanted to see.

The minute the door opened and she walked down the steps, he asked, "Where in the hell were you? I've been waiting here for two hours, waiting for every bus since six o'clock."

"Why?" she asked. "Is something wrong?"

"There's plenty wrong. Where were you?"

"I spent the day shopping in Newark and then went to a movie," she said, feeling guilty about lying but not wanting to tell him a single thing about her day.

"What did you buy? You're not carrying anything?"

"I didn't buy anything. I didn't see anything I liked."

"Who'd you go to the movies with?"

"I went by myself," she answered briskly. "Why this third degree?"

"You saw that punk again, didn't you? You're lying and you know it. Your mother told me you were meeting him. Didn't I tell you I don't want you to see him or anybody else but me? Get in the car."

"I don't want to get in the car. I want to walk home."

"I said, get in the car!" he exclaimed, grabbing her arm.

"Kenneth, stop it! I don't want to. Leave me alone or I'll—"

"You'll what? You'll do as I say, bitch. That's what you'll do. Get in the car!" he ordered again, pulling her by the arm toward the passenger side, opening up the door, and shoving her in.

She was afraid of him—the way he talked to her, his tone, his anger, his dominance. She thought she better not say anything—just let him rant and rave until she got home.

He locked her door, went around to the driver's seat, got in, started the engine, and pulled away.

"Where are we going?" she asked as he drove up the street away from Newport, which was only a block from her house. "I have to get home, Kenneth. My mother is expecting me."

"I told your mother I was going to meet you. She knows you're with me."

"But—"

"Shut up, I said. What's with you and this punk you met at the skating rink?"

"Nothing's *up*, and stop calling him that."

"I'll call him any damn thing I please. As of now, as of this very second, you're never going to see him again. Did you hear that? And you're not going to that rink again, ever. If I find out you've gone there again, I'll come there, drag you out, and crush your punk friend to pieces if he makes a move to stop me."

Kitty was furious but at the same time truly feared his rage. If only she could calm him down, get him to be reasonable. She wanted desperately to get home.

"Kenneth, please take me home," she said. "*Please!*"

"You going to listen to me?"

"Look, I don't have to listen to you. You don't own me."

"Oh, I don't, huh?" he said, reaching into his shirt pocket and taking out a cigarette. "I think I'll prove to you that I do."

He pushed in the cigarette lighter and lit the cigarette.

"Kenneth, please take me home."

"You want to go home, do you?" he asked. He took a long drag, drove into a residential street, and stopped the car short.

"What are you doing?" Kitty asked.

He grabbed her left hand. Before she had a chance to know what was happening, he bent her fingers back and stamped the lighted cigarette into her palm. Reaching over, he unlocked the door, opened it, and threw her out onto the curb.

"Walk home!" he exclaimed. "You *do* belong to me. You're wearing my brand on your palm now. Think about that."

He closed the door, started the car up, and sped

away, leaving Kitty sitting on the curb in a state of shock.

Her first reaction was to talk to her mother, but she was too confused, too humiliated even to try. She lay awake the entire night with the uncanny scene tearing through her mind. She didn't know what she was going to do. She doubted if her mother would believe her. She thought of talking to Mick about what had happened. But what could he do? She'd only involve him, which was the last thing she wanted. She figured the only out was to talk to Kenneth when she wasn't caught off guard like she was tonight, or perhaps talk it out with Kenneth and her mother together. She had to do something. She had to get out of this bizarre association as quickly and as smoothly as she could.

Kenneth can't be as crazy as he seemed to be tonight, she thought over and over again. *He can't be. How could he possibly believe that I* belong *to him?*

She didn't know what to do. But she did know she wasn't going to stop seeing Mick because Kenneth told her to. She also knew that the burning sting on her hand was the last pain she'd ever again endure from Kenneth—or anyone. It was like a hideous dream, but dreams come to an end at some point.

This was a living nightmare, all too real—one she'd have to end herself.

Kitty felt somewhat relieved that Kenneth hadn't tried to get in touch with her since Monday night. A day and a half had passed. Maybe he had gotten the message; maybe he would leave her alone! She couldn't relieve her hurt and anger, though, no matter how she tried.

"Have you heard from Kenneth?" her mother asked as they were drying the dinner dishes.

"No! And I hope I never hear from him again."

"What's the matter with you? How can you say such a thing? Kenneth's a wonderful person. He's right for you. Did the two of you have an argument? Is that why you've been sulking all day yesterday and since I came home today?"

"I don't want to go into details right now, but I know I never want to see him again."

"What happened between the two of you?"

"He's crazy, Mom. He talks crazy. He thinks he owns me, that I belong to him."

"So?"

"What do you mean, 'so'? I don't want to belong to anyone—especially him."

"O.K., what happened? He try to get fresh with you or something? All men do that, you know."

"I didn't want to tell you, but I had a bad scene with him Monday night. Look," she said, tearing the Band-Aid from her palm. "I told you I burned my hand on a pot handle. I didn't. Kenneth did this to me Monday night with a cigarette."

"Kenneth did that? It's a little hard to believe that he'd do something like that to you—or to anyone. He must've had a good reason for it. There are always two sides to a fight, you know. Tell me, what did you do to deserve his acting like that?" she asked.

"I didn't do anything."

"You must have, Kitty. But whether you did or you didn't, you'll get over it. It's only a little burn. It's just a sign of anger, that's all. It'll heal before you know it, just like you and Kenneth will heal your disagreement."

"Mother, he *burned* me. My hand's been paining me for two days."

"Make up with Kenneth and the pain will heal. You'll see. He didn't mean anything by what he did. He's a fine person."

Kitty couldn't believe what she was hearing. Her own mother rationalizing what Kenneth had done.

"Men do funny things when they're angry. You should try your best not to provoke him. He's a sensitive young man. He's only looking out for your own good."

"No matter what you say, I'm putting an end to all this. He frightens me, Mom. I hated him before, and I hate him even more now."

"You'll get over it. You'll see. In a few days the two of you will kiss and make up. That's the best part of fighting—kissing and making up. It makes up for everything, you'll see, and it'll be like nothing ever happened."

Her mother added to Kitty's confusion. Kitty realized she'd get nowhere with her and couldn't even begin to understand her mother's attitude. It was as if she were a complete stranger.

"Doris! Doris!" Grandma Perkins yelled.

"Yes, Mama," Mrs. Rhoades answered disgustedly.

"I'm going to sleep now. It's half past midnight. I have to get some sleep. Tell Billy and Kitty to come in to say good night to me."

"Billy!" Mrs. Rhoades called.

"What now?" he asked, coming from his room to the kitchen.

"Go in and say good night to Grandma."

"Good night? It's only six thirty!"

"She thinks it's later. Just do as I say and say good night to her. I'd rather she go to sleep now than call me all night. I'm sick and tired of her 'Doris, Doris,' all the time. God, I hear that voice in my sleep."

Billy looked at Kitty. She smiled at him and winked. He shrugged his shoulders as if he couldn't believe it and went into his grandmother's room.

"I've got to get going," Kitty said. "I want to get the seven o'clock bus."

"You've been going to that rink too much this summer. I'm putting a stop to it the minute school opens. No more going out on week nights. Maybe that's what Kenneth's mad about. You spend more time going and coming to that place than you do courting him. I'd be mad, too, if I were him. He's trying to offer you a future, and you're throwing it away. You'd better think yourself and your life through a little more. I don't like where your thinking is these days. Your thoughts should be with Kenneth more."

"Doris! Doris!" Grandma Perkins called again.

"Yes, Mama?"

"Kitty hasn't come in yet. Send her in to say good night to me. I need my sleep, Doris. Tell Kitty I need my sleep. It's after midnight. It might be the last night she'll have the chance to say good night to me. You never know when Daddy's coming to take me with him. Send Kitty in *now!*"

"You'd better go to her."

"I will, Mom. Sometimes I feel so sorry for her the way she's aging."

"The hell with her! Feel sorry for me once in a while and how I'm aging."

Kitty said a quick good night to Grandma Perkins, then walked to her own room, closed the door, sat down on her bed, put her hands over her face, and cried. She felt so very much alone. She couldn't wait to see Mick. She had to see him. She needed him very much.

12

"CAN I ASK YOU SOMETHING?" Mick said as they were skating.

Kitty laughed. "That's a funny question coming from you."

"What's so funny about my asking if I can ask you a question?"

"Because you're *always* asking questions. Every time we're together you ask me questions. Dozens and dozens of them. You've asked me questions since the moment we met."

"Forget it," he said, feeling somewhat put down.

"I'm sorry," she said, sensing his change of mood. "Ask me."

"I just wanted to ask if there was anything wrong, that's all. You seem different tonight, as if something's on your mind."

Kitty didn't answer.

"Well?" he pressed.

"Let's get off the floor. Let's go to our bench and talk, O.K.?"

He led her off the floor and over to what they had dubbed their "5-P bench," the bench where they had met—particular, personal, private, public place.

"Tired?" J.P. asked, sitting there sipping a Coke.

"No, we just want to talk. Get up," Mick ordered.

"What do you mean, get up? I'm sitting here, aren't I? You've got your name on this bench or something?"

"J.P., Kitty and I want to sit here and talk for a while—alone. O.K.?"

"Boy!" J.P. exclaimed. "You sure are weird sometimes. Remind me to make a reserved sign the next time I come. I'll attach it to the bench for you."

As he skated away, Kitty said, "That wasn't nice. He has a right to sit here."

"I'll apologize to him later. He won't be mad. This is *our* bench, right?"

"Right, but don't forget, the last two P's stand for 'public place.' You added that on, remember?"

"I remember."

"Do you remember the first night we met?" Kitty asked.

"Like it was a moment ago."

"You asked me dozens of questions that night. Three times within minutes you asked me if I wanted a Coke."

"I didn't know what else to say to you. Your hand bothering you, Kitty?" he asked.

"No, it's O.K."

"Be more careful when you're making soup for your grandmother next time, promise?"

"Promise."

"Now, tell me what's wrong. Did I do something or say something?"

"It has nothing to do with you, Mick. Nothing."

"Something wrong at home?"

"Everything's wrong at home, but that's not un-usual. I'd begin to get worried if everything was ever right. It's just that—"

She wanted to spill it all out, tell him everything about Kenneth, but something stopped her.

"What is it Kitty?" Mick asked.

"It's just that I have a problem that I have to solve by myself."

"Does it concern me?"

"No."

"Your family?"

"In a way. Mick, I'll talk to you about it Saturday night, O.K.? I promise. I need some time to think it all through on my own. It's nothing really serious. I shouldn't have said anything in the first place."

"Why don't you talk to me now? If something is bugging you, maybe I can help."

"Let it rest until Saturday, please?"

"Damn! I hate it when people do this to me. You

tell me there's something wrong, that you have a problem to solve, then you won't tell me what it's all about. What am I supposed to think?"

"Don't think about it at all. Forget I mentioned it —until Saturday. It's only three days away, Mick."

"You win. But I don't like it."

"Nervous about tonight?" she asked, changing the subject.

"A little. It's the first time I'm doing the routine to 'Calliope Girl' in front of the gang. It's still rough in spots. I need time to get it right."

"It'll be more than right. You'll be perfect. I can't wait for the audition to come. I think I'm looking forward to it more than you are."

"I wish you could stay to see me tonight."

"I do, too, Mick. But I have to catch the last bus home. Unfortunately they only have Wednesday night schedules on Wednesday nights."

"You still promise to stay late on Saturday? I want your opinion, Kitty. I need it. It's important to me."

"I will. I promise."

"Listen, I know it isn't easy for you, dragging yourself back and forth from Montclair to here. And I know the problems you have with your mother. Maybe it's time we got to meet one another. Maybe once she's met me she'll feel more secure. Let's arrange something soon, before the summer flies away?"

116

"All right. I'll arrange something soon."

She knew it was inevitable—that eventually Mick would have to meet her mother. She dreaded it, especially after meeting his parents. But Mick was probably right. After her mother met him, she'd feel easier about Kitty's seeing him so much. She also knew it would be easier once Kenneth was out of the picture.

"I'll give you a quarter for your thoughts," Mick said.

"A quarter? What happened to the proverbial penny?"

"It's the age of inflation. Even thoughts have gone up in price. Really, what were you thinking about?"

"About us."

"Good thinking. What about us?"

"The whole thing. Meeting you here at Wonder Wheels, getting to know you. You've changed my life in many ways in such a short time."

"Give me a chance and I'll change it even more."

"You'd better round up Jingo and Lisa. The last Trio should be coming up soon, shouldn't it? I'm going to take off my skates and get ready for my good old bus to whisk me away from you again."

"I'll walk you over to the bus stop, Kitty."

"Don't be ridiculous. It's only across the street. By the time you take off your skates and put them back on again I'll be on my way home."

"I want to. I'll skip the Trio. Jing and Lisa won't

mind. Mary Lou can skate it with them. I could use some air; the air in here gets stuffy by the end of the night. You should see me after practice. I'm like a drowned rat—drenched! Besides, it'll give me a few more minutes to be with you. That beats Trio-ing anytime. Get changed. I'll go tell Jing and Lisa and come right back. Oh, and if anyone asks you a question—any question—tell them that you belong to me."

"Don't *ever* say that to me again!" Kitty snapped.

"You said that like you really meant it, Kitty. Why did you say that?"

"I didn't mean it like it sounded."

"But you said it. You *do* belong to me, don't you?"

"I'd rather think that we belong to each other, that's all."

"Boy, something is bothering you, but I'm not going to press it any further. The fact that we be-long to *each other* is fine with me. Lucky me," he added, winking with a smile that lit up his eyes. "Lucky, lucky me."

Kitty watched him glide away. *Lucky you,* she thought to herself. *Lucky me. Lucky* us!

It was the first time in her life that she had ever felt so strongly for anyone. She was so happy when she was with Mick; she knew he felt the same way, too.

·   ·   ·

"I'm edgy about tonight," Mick said, waiting for the bus to come.

"Don't be," Kitty answered. "You'll knock 'em dead tonight with that new song. I only wish I could watch you. You'll be in my head, though. I'll close my eyes and see you. I'll be with you each and every moment. Think of me."

"I'm always thinking of you. I think about you day and night. From now until Saturday will be like an eternity. I can't even call you. It's crazy. Do you know what I did yesterday? I kept walking in the spaghetti section hoping you'd pop up again. I'm not only on edge about practicing tonight, I'm concerned over that problem of yours—the one you won't tell me about till Saturday."

"I wish I hadn't mentioned anything to you. Can you do me a big favor and forget it? Like forget I brought it up? If I hadn't, you wouldn't be concerned with it, right?"

"Right! But you did and I am. The bus is coming," he said, looking down the road where it had stopped for a light. "Why do I hate that bus so much when you leave and love it so much when it brings you to me?"

"I don't know anything about your love/hate affair with that bus. I do know that I love you."

"I love you too, Kitty. Saturday can't come fast enough."

The bus began moving. Before it pulled into the

curb, Mick added, "Take care of yourself, Kitty. Take care of that stupid burn."

"I will. Good luck tonight. See you Saturday, Mick."

She boarded the bus, took a seat, and blew him a kiss through the window.

He waited until the bus was out of sight, then made his way back across the street to Wonder Wheels, feeling an emptiness inside him that seemed to envelop his entire mind and body.

Kitty knew that feeling all too well. Each time she left Mick, she had that feeling—almost from the minute they had met.

She leaned back in her seat, rested her head against the support, and closed her eyes. All she wanted to think about was Mick—nothing else—and she did.

When the driver called, "Church Street. Next stop, Newport Road," she took her skate box, got up, and walked down the aisle.

"Rink crowded tonight?" the driver asked, noticing her skate box.

"Not too bad. It's more crowded on weekends."

"Ain't been on roller skates since I was a kid—before I went in the army. Good to know kids are still skatin' today. Newport," he called. "Guess this is your stop."

"Yes, thank you," she said and walked off the bus. "Good night."

"Good night now. See ya again soon, I hope."

"Thanks again," Kitty called.

Turning to a passenger directly behind him, he said, "Now there's a nice kid. Can't tell me all teenagers are bad. There are still some kids brought up with manners. Ain't all delinquents."

She hadn't walked more than half a block before Kenneth's car pulled up alongside her and stopped. For a second she was both surprised and terrified, but she decided that she'd be strong with him for once. If he dared try anything like he did on Monday night . . .

"Get in the car, Kitty," Kenneth said. "I'll drive you home and we can talk."

"Kenneth, I don't want any more scenes. I want to walk home. Call me tomorrow and we'll talk on the phone, O.K.?"

"That's ridiculous. Get in so we can talk now."

"Kenneth, I want to walk home. Please leave me alone. I really don't want to talk to you or anyone tonight."

She started walking faster, wanting to run but knowing he might sense she was scared of him. That was the last thing she wanted.

He started the car up again. Cruising alongside her, he said again, "Get in. Get in this car right now or I'm going to have to force you."

She ignored him and continued walking.

The anger in him rose to the boiling point. He slammed on the brake, got out, and grabbed her arm.

"Kenneth, stop it! Let go of me!" she pleaded.

"You were screwin' around with that guy again, weren't you? Didn't I tell you I didn't want you to see him again? Didn't I?"

"Kenneth, please let go of me. I want to talk to you, but not now. I'm too upset over what happened Monday and I don't want another scene. Just let me go home, *please*?"

He pulled her toward the car and tried to push her inside. She swung her skate box around and hit him in the knee.

He grabbed her again, harder than before, took the skate box from her, shoved her in, locked her door, and got in himself.

"That's the last time you'll ever hit me, you little bitch. Tramp-whore! This is the end of your seeing that punk at the rink, too."

Kitty was terrified. He was like a madman. She bit her lower lip to try to keep from crying. It didn't help. Tears streamed down her face. He continued to rant and rave, calling her all kinds of terrible names.

Thoughts flashed through her confused and frightened mind. She thought of the way her father used to abuse her mother; she thought about her mother; she thought about Mick.

Suddenly she realized Kenneth was not driving in the direction of her house.

"Where are you going?" she asked, nearly hysterical. "Let me out of this car. I want to go home."

"You're going to my house. If it takes all night, I'm not going to let you out of my sight. I'm going to teach you some sense about life. You're mine. All mine. You belong to me. Can't you get that through your thick skull? If I can't have you, no son-of-a-bitch teen-aged punk will either."

Screaming at the top of his lungs he continued to yell, "Mine, mine, mine! You're mine!"

Kitty prayed for this unbelievable ordeal to end.

13

"MOM!" MICK SHOUTED, coming in from work.

"I'm out here, Mick," she answered from the backyard.

"Hi," he said. "What are you doing?"

"Weeding this flowerbed of zinnias. I never saw so many weeds. It's becoming a full-time job. I get more weeds than I do zinnias!"

"It's kind of hot to do that now. Wait till it gets cooler and I'll help you."

"I'm stopping. It is too hot. Phew! Did you remember to bring home the cold cuts?" she asked, taking off her gardening gloves and plopping into a chair.

"Of course I remembered. I put them in the refrigerator. What time will Dad be home?"

"Late tonight. He has a dinner meeting after

work. He said he'd try to catch the eight seventeen train. Looks as if you and me will be cold-cutting alone. How was work today?"

"All right," he answered, stretching out on the grass beside her chair.

"You really don't like it, do you?"

"Not really. There's nothing much to like about it."

"In another month it'll be all over. The summer seems to be racing by, doesn't it? The audition will be here before you know it. How did the routine go last night."

"O.K."

"Just O.K.?"

"I'd say less than O.K."

"Doesn't the music work as well as you thought it would?"

"The song is great. It's just that I wasn't."

"What did Ange say?"

"Ange always says the same thing: 'Great, great!' But *I* know I wasn't. I had some trouble with a leap I put in between a triple spin."

"Maybe you're trying too hard."

"I am trying too hard. And I'm going to try harder until I get it perfect. If it doesn't work by the night of the audition I can always drop it out. But it's so effective."

"Kitty was there last night, too, wasn't she?"

"Yeah."

"What did she say?"

"She couldn't stay that late. She has to depend on bus schedules. The stupid last bus runs earlier during the week than on Saturday nights. In a way I'm glad she didn't stay. She'll watch me Saturday night. I'm going to practice late tomorrow night. Lisa is staying, too. Ange is letting me lock up."

"How is she doing?"

"Lisa? She's great, Mom. Really beautiful. There's no way she won't win in the audition. She's really got it all together."

"It would be great if the two of you were together next summer. At least then you wouldn't feel like a stranger in Paradise Lane."

Mick laughed.

"What's so funny?" Jessica asked.

"Do you realize what you just said: A stranger in Paradise—like the song, get it?"

"I got it, but I wish I had realized I was being punny. Remember to tell that gem to your father. He loves corn at its ripest! Listen, I had an idea. Why don't we have a party here over Labor Day weekend, to celebrate?"

"Celebrate what?"

"We can celebrate a million things. We can celebrate the end of summer, the end for you at Foods-For-You, and, of course, you and possibly Lisa winning in the audition."

"And what if we don't win?"

"Then we can celebrate the fact that it's all over. We can sit around depressed and curse out the big wheels at Paradise Lane, U.S.A., for not recognizing talent. Will it bother you if you don't win, Mick? Mick?"

"Of course it will, Mom. You know how much I want to win. Where would I ever get another opportunity like this? I won't be depressed or anything like that if I don't win. Believe me, I won't commit suicide."

"Well, that's good to know! What do you think of my idea?"

"The party? It sounds like fun. How many people would we have?"

"As many as you want. We'll have a barbecue. You know how much your father loves to cook. We'll invite all the kids—Lisa, Jingo, Mary Lou . . ."

"And Kitty, of course. She's number one on the list—any list."

"Oh, she is, is she?"

"Yeah, *numerale uno*," he said, closing his eyes, smiling, picturing her face in his mind.

"You two are really hung up on each other, aren't you?"

"Kind of. Mom, when *do* you know? How do you know when it's right?"

"You just know, that's all."

"But I've only known Kitty for a little while."

"There's no such thing as a little while when two

people know a relationship is right. It only takes a moment, sometimes a glance, a meeting of the eyes, a first touch to know. And you never forget it, either. Eighteen years ago, on May third at four o'clock in the afternoon, the first time I saw your father, I knew. So did he. He was working part-time at a soda fountain. I remember it like it happened five seconds ago. Kitty might be the first of many girls you'll feel strongly about. But you'll never forget the first time, or her. If it does happen again, and I'm sure it will, you'll sense it. It'll be different each time, but you'll know."

"How would you know? You and Dad were married a year after you met?"

"I had boy friends before him. Do you think your generation discovered love? If you did, none of you would be around right now. Let's get back to the party. Would you like to invite anyone from the supermarket?"

"No way. I see enough of them."

"Do you think Kitty's mother and brother would like to come? That way, she could drive her here."

"I don't know. I'd have to ask Kitty. She doesn't seem to be too fond of her mother."

"How can you say such a thing?"

"Well, there's always something screwy going on in her house. I told you about her situation. She doesn't relate to her mother."

"I hate to sound like an amateur psychologist, but

128

that isn't unusual. Many kids in their teens go through that, feeling as if their parents are merely an enormous pain in their life."

"I didn't go through it."

"You're different."

"How?"

"Come on, Mick. You can't compare your life to others, especially Kitty's. For the most part, you've had smooth sailing all your life. We might have a different relationship, too, if we went through a divorce. It's natural. Something like that can turn your whole life upside down and inside out. The next time you see Kitty, ask her. Let's invite Angelo, too. He's done a lot for you."

"And Ro. Let's have Ro," Mick added. "She's great and adds fun to anything."

"Of course we'll invite her. She is fun."

"Can I ask you something?" he said, getting up off the grass.

"What?"

"Look at me," he said, turning around slowly.

"Yes?"

"Notice anything?"

"Yes, your shirt's all wrinkled."

"Look lower—at my buns. Notice anything?"

"Yes, you've got grass stains on your behind."

"Nothing else?"

"O.K., it's time to stop the guessing game. What am I supposed to notice?"

"My underwear. Do my boxer shorts sag under my jeans?"

"Well, now that you've told me, yes they do. But why are you asking me this in the middle of planning a guest list?"

"Ro told me about them. She told me to change my underwear—to go from boxers to jockey shorts —especially for the audition."

"I don't know what's going on these days at Wonder Wheels. What is Rosemary doing looking at your, uh, as you call them, buns, may I ask?"

"She just noticed it, that's all. She sees everything from the organ rise."

"To say the least! Want me to pick you up a few pair of jockey shorts? I'll be downtown Saturday and I'll get them for you then."

"No way. Methinks I'm old enough to pick out my own underwear. I'll get them before the audition. Hey, you forgot someone."

"Who?"

"J.P."

"I didn't forget J.P. I consider him a fixture—part of the family."

"That part of the family is coming over tonight about eight o'clock and I have some things I have to do after supper. Let's go in and make sandwiches. I'm starving."

"Me, too," Jessica said. "Let's go."

. . .

"You make the best lemonade in the world," Mick said, sipping it through a straw from a long, tall glass.

"I owe that to your father. *He* makes the best lemonade in the world. He always tells me that the two best things he found as a part-time soda jerk was this recipe for lemonade and me—in that order!"

"Mick! *Mick!*" J.P. called.

"Is that J.P.?" asked Jessica.

"It shouldn't be, but it must be. It's only seven fifteen. He must've gotten away from the record shop early."

"Mick! *Mick!* Let me in, please. *Please!*"

"I'm coming, J.P. Don't get so uptight."

"The screen door's locked. Let me in!"

"Calm down, man. You sound as if a panther is chasing you. What's up?" he asked, unlatching the door.

Instead of bursting into the house as he usually did, J.P. stood in the doorway looking ghostly white, clutching a newspaper under his arm.

"What's the matter? You look funny. Come on in."

"Is it J.P.?" Jessica called.

"Yeah, Mom."

J.P.'s hands began to shake; his eyes welled up

131

with tears. "You didn't hear, did you?" he asked. "You didn't see the paper?"

"Hear and see what? What's the matter?" Mick asked, becoming anxious. "Don't tell me another President was shot."

"Worse. It's worse. It's Kitty," he said, handing him the folded-over newspaper.

Mick grabbed the paper from him and began reading a headline on the second page: *Couple Found Dead In Car.*

Two Montclair residents, Kitty Elizabeth Rhoades, 17, and Kenneth Barret Delaney, 20, were found dead this morning from carbon monoxide poisoning shortly before 9:00 a.m. by young Delaney's parents in a car parked in the Delaney garage at 411 Summer Avenue. . . .

Mick sank down on the sofa and read the first sentence again and again.

"It's terrible, isn't it?" J.P. asked, crying.

Mick didn't answer. He was dazed. It was as if someone had knocked the life out of him with a sledgehammer.

Calling in from the kitchen, Jessica said, "Hi, J.P. Come on out for a sec and see what I made especially for you."

He walked slowly into the kitchen.

132

"What's the matter?" Jessica asked, seeing how distraught he looked.

"It's Kitty, Mrs. Thompson. She's dead."

"*What?*" she screamed, running into the living room. "Is this a joke or something?" she said to Mick. "If this is a joke, it's sick."

"It's true, Mom," Mick answered, handing her the newspaper, dazed.

Jessica took it and read the complete article:

Two Montclair residents, Kitty Elizabeth Rhoades, 17, and Kenneth Barret Delaney, 20, were found dead this morning from carbon monoxide poisoning shortly before 9:00 a.m. by young Delaney's parents in a car parked in the Delaney garage at 411 Summer Avenue.

The couple apparently died accidentally at about midnight last night.

The car's engine was running and the vehicle and garage were filled with exhaust fumes when the bodies were found by Mr. Delaney.

Kitty Rhoades, about to enter her senior year at Thomas Jefferson High School in Montclair, New Jersey, is survived by her mother, Doris, a brother, Billy, and a grandmother. Delaney, an assistant manager at Macy's in Roselle Shopping Center, is survived by his parents.

When police arrived on the scene, they found the couple sitting next to one another on the car's front seat. All the car windows were closed and the car doors were locked. The County Medical Examiner, who will perform the autopsies, pronounced the couple dead at 8:46 a.m. Police did not know how long the couple had been sitting in the car.

Both Miss Rhoades and Mr. Delaney were parishioners at the Mount Sinai Presbyterian Church in Montclair.

Funeral services will be held separately. Miss Rhoades will repose at the Marshall Funeral Home at 15 Church Street in Montclair on Saturday. Visiting hours are 10:00 a.m. to 5:00 p.m. Funeral services will be held at Mount Olympus Cemetery on Sunday morning.

Mr. Delaney will repose . . .

"I can't believe this," said Jessica. "I can't. It's impossible. Who is Kenneth Delaney?"

Mick didn't answer.

"My God. It can't be true. It just can't be," Jessica kept saying. "Mick, say something! Say anything. *Please?*"

He couldn't.

She walked over to the sofa, sat down beside Mick, and held his hand, squeezing it tighter and tighter. J.P. came in and sat with them; tears were streaming down his face.

Jessica put her arm around him, nestling his wet face on her shoulder. The three of them stared silently at the newspaper in total disbelief until J.P. broke the silence.

"Poor Kitty," he said. "How could this happen to her? She was so good. How could it happen, Mrs. Thompson? How?"

14

"HAVE A CUP of coffee with me, Mick."

"Sure, Mom," he said, sitting down at the table.

As she poured the coffee, Jessica asked him, "Do you still think it's a good idea to go there alone?"

"Yes, I really do. I've given it a lot of thought, Mom. I talked with Dad for hours last night, and what he says is right. It would be stupid and unnecessary to get further involved, or involve anyone else in this, especially after I spoke on the telephone with Billy. The whole thing is an unbelievable mess. There are moments when I can't believe it. I just can't. I saw Kitty Wednesday night, Thursday I found out about it, and tomorrow morning she's going to be buried. It just doesn't seem possible—or fair."

"I know it doesn't. I can't believe it either."

"How could her mother not know she didn't come home?"

"Didn't Billy explain that?"

"He explained a lot of things—the best he could. Their mother leaves the house early every day. But wouldn't you think she'd look in to see if everyone was there and all right? Especially with her own mother so old and sick?"

"It's not impossible, Mick. At times I leave the house in the morning without disturbing you. That can easily happen."

"I feel so sorry for that little kid. He found out when the police called the house. He told me he ran into Kitty's room. Her bed was still made. It was then that he realized all this was for real. What a shock to lay on a kid."

"It's a tragic waste of two young lives."

"You know, Mom, it's funny. I don't feel anything about Kenneth. All he does is confuse the picture. Why didn't Kitty tell me about him? Why did she see him after she left the rink on Wednesday? I knew something was wrong Wednesday night. She told me she had a problem of some kind, that she wanted to work it out by herself, that she'd tell me about it—ha!—tonight! It had to have something to do with that guy. It had to. Billy said they knew each other for a long time from church—she hated him, but her mother thought a lot of him. Why didn't she tell me about him? Why?"

"I don't have answers to any of this, Mick. The best thing to do is try to forget all that. Otherwise, it will drive you crazy. Kitty must have had her own private reasons for not telling you about him. You're going to have to get through this mess and let time work it away. What happened is horrible. We'll never forget it. But time will put it in some kind of perspective. I still don't like the idea of your facing this alone this morning. I wish you'd let J.P. or Jingo take you. Or reconsider my driving you there."

"I asked the kids not to go. The last thing I want is to be surrounded by Lisa and Jing and the gang. I want to see Kitty for the last time by myself. Dad agrees with me. He even called the funeral parlor and asked if I could come in today before ten o'clock. He is right about me not having to meet all those relatives and strangers, and he's right about me not going to the cemetery tomorrow. No one even knows who I am, except Billy, and it wouldn't do Kitty any good. Nothing matters now."

"What time do you have to get the bus?"

"Soon. I better get moving."

"Do you have the address?"

"Yeah, some bargain."

"Come on. I'll drive you up to the bus stop."

"You don't have to. I'll walk. I have time."

"I want to. I'll get the car keys."

She left the kitchen. Mick stared into his empty coffee cup. Empty! he thought to himself. A few minutes ago you were full—brewing and steaming with life. Now you're empty. Things can become empty so fast in life. So damned fast!

He felt odd riding the bus—this bus, Kitty's bus. He wondered what Kitty thought about as she rode back and forth. He wondered if she had ever sat on this particular bus or even in this very same seat. He thought about Billy and about Kenneth—who he was and why Kitty met him Wednesday night if she hated him. And he thought and thought about Kitty. There were so many unanswered questions.

"Tree Lane Drive," the driver called. "This stop is Tree Lane Drive. Church Street is the next stop."

Mick pulled the cord to signal the driver that he was getting off and started walking down the aisle.

"Can you tell me which direction number fifteen Church is, sir?"

"Number fifteen should be in the middle of the block. Just walk up and you'll find it easily. You're a tall drink of water, son," he said, smiling.

Mick smiled back weakly.

"Church Street," he called. "This is your stop. Just walk up Church and you'll bump right into number fifteen."

"Thank you very much. 'Bye now."

" 'Bye. See you again soon, I hope."

"Thanks again," Mick added, walking off the bus.

"Nice kids," the driver said to a passenger behind him. "Nice kids on this route. Can't tell me all teenagers are bad. I always say there are still some kids brought up with manners. Ain't all delinquents."

The Marshall Funeral Home was easy to find. Too easy. Mick wished it hadn't been. Next to it was a small florist. Almost as if it was an automatic move, Mick walked in.

"Beautiful day, isn't it?" a woman asked as he entered. "Too beautiful for words. What can I do for you?"

"I'd like one rose," he said.

"Red or yellow?" she asked.

"Uh, yellow," he answered.

"Do you want it in bud or opened?"

"Opened, please."

The woman went to a refrigerated case and took out an opened yellow rose.

"How's this?" she asked. "Isn't this a beauty?"

"Yes, it's fine, maam."

"For your mother?"

"No, a friend."

"That's nice. Lucky girl. This beauty will certainly brighten up her day. I always say there's nothing like flowers to brighten up a day. That's why I'm in this business. Let's see, that'll be one dollar and fifty cents," she said, "plus eight cents tax. One dollar and fifty-eight cents."

As he placed the money on the counter she put a piece of white tissue paper loosely over the rose, carefully stapling the bottom together.

"Thank you. Come back soon. Have a great day," she said as he left the shop.

He walked next door and stood in front of the Marshall Funeral Home. A glass-encased sign read:

Reposing Today Are:

Elmira Weeks
Jonathan Seldes
Kitty Roades

The name blared out at him. He immediately noticed *Roades* was spelled wrong. As he walked up the stairs he took a deep breath. He wanted so much to see Kitty and at the same time he was terrified.

A small, bald-headed man dressed in a black suit, white shirt, and black tie was sitting behind the desk.

"Hello," Mick said.

"Good morning," the man answered. "I'm Mr. Briggs. We don't open for another forty-five minutes or so. What can I do for you?"

"I'm here to see Kitty Rhoades. My father called last night and someone said it would be all right if I came early for a few minutes."

"Oh, yes," Mr. Briggs answered. "I was that someone. I'm the manager. You a relative of the girl?"

"No, a friend. A special friend."

"Shame she's so young. Youngest I've had in here for quite a long time."

"You have her name spelled wrong on the sign outside," Mick told him. "There's an *h* in it. It's R-*h*-o-a-d-e-s."

"I'd fix it, but she'll be out of here tomorrow already. They come and go fast these days. Used to lay out three days—sometimes longer. Wait here a minute and let me check to see if everything is in order. Be right back."

Mick noticed the smell of flowers permeating the place. At first the scent seemed sweet and pleasurable, but it quickly turned acrid, almost bitterly repulsive, making him somewhat heady. He looked at the rose and wondered why he had bought it. He didn't even know if Kitty liked roses. He thought of chucking it into the wastebasket alongside the desk, but Mr. Briggs was returning, causing the thought to flee.

"You can go in now. Miss Rhoades is in Parlor C, down the hall, first door on your left."

"Thank you," Mick answered, starting down the hall.

"Oh," called Mr. Briggs. "Do you want some music?"

"Music?" Mick asked confused.

"Organ music. People like the effect that music

gives. Helps some grieve lighter. Don't usually pipe it into the rooms until about five minutes before opening. But I'll put it on for you if you like."

"No, thanks," Mick said, wondering how anyone could be in this cold and dreary business.

As he walked down the hall his legs shook, nearly buckling. Entering the parlor, he saw Kitty lying in the casket. He walked over and stared at her. Her body looked so small in the wooden coffin with white satin puffed up all around her. The silence in the room was unbearable; the scent of flowers sickening.

He knelt down on the small prayer bench in front of the coffin and continued staring. He wanted to cry, but wouldn't. He didn't want Kitty to see him like that. He knew she couldn't see him, but he prayed that somehow she could sense that he was there—with her, by her side.

People always said that the dead looked as if they were merely sleeping. Kitty didn't look like that at all to Mick. She looked peaceful, but she looked dead. Her cheeks were a little puffy, and the lights glaring down gave her an almost plastic-looking appearance.

"I've got a lot to tell you, Kitty," he whispered to her. "Yet I don't know what to say. I miss you. I miss you so very much. I want to skate the next Couples Only with you at Wonder Wheels—every Couples Only. I want to hear your laugh, and I want to ask

143

you a few thousand more of my silly questions, even though I know I'm always asking you questions."

He began to shake. As much as he tried, he couldn't help but cry. Tears streamed down his cheeks and on to the arm he rested on the coffin. He wiped his eyes on his sleeve. His skin felt tight where the tears had dried. He took a deep breath. He wanted to stay with her forever; he also wanted to get away.

He gently unfastened the staples from the tissue paper covering the rose.

"We never talked about flowers, Kitty. There's so much we never got the chance to talk about. I don't even know if you like roses. I don't know why I bought it, but I want you to know you have something from me—if only for a little while."

Gently he lifted her hand, put the yellow rose in it, and placed it back down on her chest.

"I'm going to go now, Kitty. Sleep well. My meeting you was the greatest thing that ever happened to me. You'll always be in my heart and thoughts and prayers. Always."

He stood up, bent over her, kissed her on the forehead, and gently stroked her soft brown hair.

" 'Bye, girl. I love you. I love you, Kitty—more than life itself."

15

WONDER WHEELS TEEMED WITH PEOPLE—people who had never been there before. If Angelo was ever right about anything, he was right about the draw the Paradise Lane, U.S.A., auditions was to the rink.

Although the auditions were set to begin at eight p.m. *sharp*, as it said in the rules, it wasn't until nine fifteen that things got under way.

A large rectangular table was set up on the floor of the rink directly under the organ rise. Behind it, a young woman sat busily shuffling papers and playing with a Polaroid camera; next to her sat Lloyd Jamison, audition manager for Paradise Lane. To his left was a man who sat doing nothing; he looked more bored with the entire procedure than anyone could possibly look.

Mr. Jamison had already given the crowd a pep

talk about "the quality of talent" he was looking for and reviewed the basic rules with some thirty people who were going to audition. He was short, forty-ish, but looked as if he tried hard to appear as if he were still in his teens. An ostentatious gold medallion hung down over his unbuttoned silk shirt. His outfit was completed by too-tight jeans and tennis shoes.

"Silence, please," he bellowed into a hand microphone. He reminded Mick of Murph. "We're ready to begin the Preliminary Skate. In five minutes all of those who signed up will be asked to do a Preliminary Skate for about ten minutes. This will give my colleagues and I a chance to look for a variety of things. Just skate naturally—by yourself. This is *not* the time to show off. Save that for the individual competition.

"All we're looking for now is height, weight, movement, et cetera, et cetera. Following that your number will be called to give you an opportunity to do your stuff. You'll have at least a fifteen-minute break to change into costumes and get your music together, et cetera, et cetera. Are there any questions?"

Before anyone could possibly even raise a hand, he added, "Good! And remember to be on the floor can't wait for you or begin looking for you. You have *on time*—as soon as your number is called. We to learn fast that punctuality is a prime ingredient in show biz. If you don't learn that, you're through with a capital *TH*."

"You O.K.?" Lisa asked Mick.

"I'm fine, Lisa."

"Nervous?" she asked.

"No, funny enough. You?"

"Not yet. I'd just like this whole thing to get over with. It's endless."

"I know, but Ange said it's normal for them to take so much time. He told me that the judges will eliminate at least half on the Preliminary Skate. He said they really know what they're after."

"Let me fix your number, Mick. It's lopsided."

Lisa straightened the card on Mick's back, which had a huge number forty-one printed on it. Lisa's number was thirty-four.

"Thanks, Lisa," he said.

"By the way, where is Ange?" she asked. "I haven't seen him for a while."

"Ange is going crazy. He's over filling the Coke machine again. It's the third time tonight. He said he's going to run out of everything if this doesn't get started soon. You ever see so many people?"

"No, it's incredible, isn't it?"

"Who's that little kid?" he asked, pointing to a girl of about nine sitting quietly beside her mother.

"I don't know, but she's auditioning. She's wearing number twenty-seven."

"Ever see her before?"

"No."

"She's cute. They're growing skaters younger these days. Oh, by the way, Mary Lou raved over your outfit. I can't wait to see it."

"J.P. told me yours was dynamite, too."

The ten-minute Preliminary Skate lasted for about fifteen minutes.

"What are they doing now?" Lisa asked, skating closer to Mick.

"Who knows? Hey, look at number twenty-seven. She's great. I'm going over to introduce myself. Hi," he said, skating close to her. "What's your name?"

"Jodi," she answered. "Jodi Joyce Rossi."

"I'm Mick. Mick Thompson. Ever come to Wonder Wheels before?"

"Uh-uh. I skate in Somerset at Dreamland. I want to be a skater when I grow up. I've been skating all my life."

Mick laughed. "Good luck to you, Jodi Joyce Rossi," he said.

"You too," she answered nonchalantly and skated away.

After a few minutes the taped music ended abruptly.

"Thank you," Jamison called. "In fifteen minutes we'll start with numbers twenty through thirty."

J.P. ran over to Lisa and Mick. "Ange wants to see both of you," he said. "Right now. He went to his office with Ro. Why didn't either of you *do* anything out there? All you did was skate!"

"That's all we were told to do, J.P.," said Lisa.

"Yeah, I know, but couldn't you have impressed them a little? Couldn't you have done at least a *few* groovy steps? You should've done a spin or something, Mick, or a—"

"Cool down. There's time for that J.P.," Mick answered. "Let's see what Ange wants. We have to get into our outfits. Did you check the tapes, J.P.?"

"I've got both yours and Lisa's cassette set up and ready to spin. Don't worry about it. Concentrate on your routines."

"Ange?" J.P. called, knocking on his office door. "Mick and Lisa are here."

"Come on in. Door's open."

"How's it going, Ro?" Mick asked.

"It's O.K. From what I just saw out there you two are shoe-ins. Natural shoe-ins."

"What did you want, Ange?"

"Look!" he said, pointing to two supply-room doors.

"Surprise! Surprise!" Rosemary shouted.

On each door was a large star cut from gold-colored metallic paper; one reading *Lisa,* the other, *Mick.*

"Private dressing rooms—only for my Wonder Wheels regulars," said Angelo.

Lisa looked at Mick. Neither could believe it.

"You think I'd have *my* stars change in toilets with the common herd? No way. Use these rooms to change and relax in. Ro will come and get you just before your numbers are called."

"That's nice of you to do, Ange. Thanks," Mick said.

"Thanks, Ange," said Lisa, going over to him and planting a kiss on his bald head.

"No need for thanks or kisses. Just win! That'll thank me for everything. If you win, you can keep the star. You can put it on your skate box. But I'm warning you, if you *don't* win, I'm taking it back and saving it until the next time Wonder Wheels has auditions."

"We'd better get our outfits, Mick," Lisa said.

"Your stuff's already in there," said J.P. "Mary Lou and I rounded everything up for you."

"Where is Mary Lou?" Lisa asked. "She's going to help me change."

"On the phone," Rosemary answered. "She went to call Jingo."

"Damn! I wish he could have been here tonight," Mick said. "I still can't believe he has the measles! It's really the craziest thing I ever heard. What if it happened to me or to you, Lisa?"

"It's luck, I guess. Just plain luck. It's good he's not auditioning tonight. But I miss his not being here, too."

"Not as much as Mary Lou does," Rosemary said.

"When she doesn't see him for a day she needs in-sulin to keep her blood moving through her veins."

"Oh, by the way," she added as Lisa went to her room. "I'm disappointed in one thing, Mick."

"What's that?"

"You *didn't* listen to Rosemary. You still hang."

"The shorts!" Mick exclaimed. "I forgot, Ro. I really did."

"Just remember, if you lose you can blame it on your buns! You better go in and get beautiful. I'll be back," she said. "Ta-ta for now."

As Mick walked into his room he noticed a pack-age on the chair wrapped in Wonder Wheels colors, red and yellow, with a big bow on top and a card that read: *To Mick*.

He opened the card. It said: "Here's for luck, Tiger. Love 'n' kisses. Ro."

He tore open the wrapping and laughed loudly. It was a pair of white nylon jockey shorts.

"Mick? Near ready?" Lisa called.

"In a minute, Lisa."

"What do you think is going on out there?"

"I don't know. All I can hear is music stopping and starting."

"Where is everybody?"

"Watching, I guess. J.P. said the auditions started, but that was ten minutes ago. O.K., I'm ready," he called, brushing his hair, setting loose strands in place with his fingers. He walked out of the room and sat down behind Angelo's desk to put on his show skates.

"*Da-da!*" Lisa announced, coming out of her room.

"God! You look gorgeous, Lisa. You really look gorgeous."

"You like it?" she asked, twirling around.

"Fantastic! Just fantastic!"

"My aunt made it," she said. "It's all done in old patches."

"The colors are great. All I can say is that you look great-plus."

"Thanks, Mick," she said. "Stand up."

He rolled from behind the desk.

"Wow!" she exclaimed. "You're magical."

"Like it?" he asked.

"You're beautiful—I mean handsome—no, beautiful. Beautiful is the only word I can use to describe how you look tonight."

"Well, well, well," Rosemary said, coming in. "Wonder Wheels treasures. You're both knockouts. Turn around, both of you. Knockouts! Aw, I see you got my little present, Mick."

"You really notice that I have them on?" he asked smiling.

"Of course I do. What an improvement! You see, the old gal isn't so dumb after all, is she?"

"What's the big secret?" Lisa asked.

"Tell her later," Rosemary said. "Lisa, you're on in a few minutes. J.P.'s all ready, that is if he doesn't

152

have a sugar fit. So far he's had three Cokes and two ice-cream bars."

"Where's Ange?" Mick asked.

"He's already at the light bar. Remember, he's giving you three spots, Lisa. Try to wind up in the center. Mick, you'll have the strobe globe, just like you practiced with. The lights will really add a lot to your routines, not that either of you need them."

"How's it going out there, Ro?" Mick asked.

"The Paradise Lane, U.S.A., group isn't too excited. Not that I blame them. There's not too much talent out there. Most have been eliminated. There was only one callback, number twenty-seven. A little tyke who's very good for her age."

"Great, that's Jodi," Mick said.

"Oh? Don't be too excited. If you lose out to what I think is a fifty-year-old midget passing off as a kid, I'll faint and never recover! Come on. Let's go," she said.

Lisa started for the door.

"Wait a minute, Lisa," Mick called. "Ro, mind if we have a few seconds together?"

"Not at all. But no more than just a few. Remember," she added, imitating Jamison's tone of voice, "punctuality is a prime ingredient in show biz, *et cetera, et cetera.*"

She left the room, closing the door behind her.

"I just wanted to wish you luck, Lisa."

"Thanks, Mick. You know I wish you the same."

"Thanks for helping me through the past few weeks, too. You'll never know how much I appreciate it all."

"Let's not talk about it now, Mick. Let's just concentrate on getting through these next few minutes."

He hugged her for a second, then said, "Let's go. Let's get this over with."

"Thank you," Jamison called to someone who looked quite disappointed, stopping him before he had the chance to complete whatever he was trying to do. "Ready for number thirty-four."

"Luck again," Mick said.

"I'm dying," Lisa replied. "All of a sudden I'm a nervous wreck."

She rolled into the center of the rink. Angelo dimmed the lights, hitting her with a center spot. J.P. started her cassette, and she began skating.

Lisa was spectacular. Within seconds after she began, a hush came over the entire rink. Mick looked over at the table. The woman was busily snapping shot after shot of her with the Polaroid. When Lisa finished her ballet in the center spotlight, there was a burst of applause.

"Number thirty-four, would you come to the table?" Jamison called, adding, "Number forty-one's next. Is forty-one ready?"

154

"I'm here," Mick said.

"Sorry you have to be last," Jamison said, "but someone has to be last. How tall are you, kid?"

"Six-one," Mick answered.

"Thank you. When you're ready, we are."

"O.K., J.P.?" Mick called over.

"O.K.," he answered. "Good luck."

He took his stance to begin his routine to "Calliope Girl." As the lights began to dim and the strobe globe started revolving, he looked over to where his mother and father were sitting. His mother blew him a kiss; his father held up and waved two crossed fingers for luck.

Before J.P. began the cassette, Mick threw back his head, closed his eyes tightly, and said to himself, "Be with me, Kitty. *Please* be with me."

There was no doubt in anybody's mind that they were watching a genius on wheels. His movements were perfection; body parts worked together as if they were being manipulated by a master puppeteer.

Twice during the routine when he spun and leaped, simultaneous rounds of applause filled the room. Jamison's assistant snapped picture after picture. Everything was right—the music provided him with every step he had been practicing for months; the colored dots of lights bouncing from the strobe globe around his beige outfit made him a kaleidoscope of dancing colors.

On the last chorus of the song, Mick went into

his spinning, moving so fast that all one could see was a blur of rainbow motion.

When he finished, bedlam broke out at the rink. People ran up to him, engulfing him in a circle. It was so loud that no one even heard Jamison call for number forty-one to come to the table.

He had done it. He knew it. He was dazzled and dazed by the response.

16

WHEN THE EXCITEMENT in the crowd began ebbing, Mick's mother and father walked over to him.

"I'm so proud of you, son, I could burst," David said.

"Thanks, Dad."

"I never knew you were *that* good," Jessica added. "You're absolutely fantastic."

"You sure you're not up to a little celebration?" his father asked.

"I'm really beat, Dad. I just want to cool off and unwind here for a while. I'd rather do that than go out tonight."

"It's your night," he said. "I can understand your wanting to be by yourself for a while. Try not to make it too late, though. You worked hard tonight."

"I'm exhausted from the tension," Jessica said, dabbing beads of sweat from Mick's forehead with her handkerchief. "I'm still in a state of shock over your skating. What did the man have to say to you?"

"He was cool. He didn't seem that impressed. He gave Lisa and me a lot of forms to fill out. All he really said was that he'd be in touch with us on Monday morning and that we're both in for next season at Paradise Lane."

"Well, that's enough, isn't it?" she asked.

"I suppose so, Mom. It all seems anticlimactic at this point. I'm glad it's over."

Lisa walked over to where they were standing.

"Congratulations, Lisa," David and Jessica both said.

"Thanks, Mr. and Mrs. Thompson."

"You positive you don't want to go to Pop's Pizza with Mary Lou and me?" she asked Mick.

"Not tonight, Lisa. I'd vomit if I had to eat pizza."

"Will you call me tomorrow?"

"Sure, I'll call you about noon, O.K.? Congrats again."

"Thanks, the best part of the whole thing is that we'll be together next summer. It will give me something to look forward to. Good night, Mr. and Mrs. Thompson."

"Good night, Lisa," they said.

" 'Bye, Mick. I'll hear from you tomorrow."

"Good night, Lisa."

"We're going, too, honey. Don't stay out too late."

"Don't wait up for me. I have my keys. J.P. and I might just drive around a little. See you in the morning."

"Night, champ," his father said, hugging his shoulders.

"Night, Dad. Night, Mom."

"Good night, Mick. We love you. We're both so proud of you."

"Well, it's over, my lovely," Rosemary said on her way out. "Wonder Wheels will never be the same again. If this old gal plays the organ up there till I'm one hundred and twenty, I'll never see skating like I did tonight."

Mick felt a tug on his sleeve. It was Jodi.

"You're a good skater," she said. "When I grow up I want to be as good as you are."

"Hey, you're already good. Congrats on winning. I'll see you next summer at Paradise Lane."

"O.K.," she answered. "I'll like that. You're cute." Turning toward Rosemary she added, "Good night, lady."

"Good night, dearie," Rosemary said, and as she walked away, exclaimed, "Midget! She's really a midget. I just know she is."

"Thanks again for the present, Ro," Mick said.

"My pleasure! Good night, Tiger."

"Good night, Ro. Ro? Thanks again—for everything."

"No need for that. Old Rosemary loves you like a son. See you next week."

"You going to change now?" J.P. asked, clutching the cassette player and tapes. "I want to get out of this place. I feel like I live here."

"I'm staying awhile, J.P. You go on home."

"How will you get home?"

"I'll walk. I really want to."

"You sure?"

"Positive."

"O.K. I'll see you tomorrow. Did your mom tell you she invited me over for breakfast? Pancakes!"

"She told me. See you about nine."

"You bet. I wouldn't miss your mother's pancakes for the world. Good night, buddy. I guess you're sick of hearing it, but congratulations from little old me."

"Thanks, J.P. I never get sick of hearing that. And thanks for everything. You helped me win tonight more than you'll ever know. 'Calliope Girl' was perfect. Thanks again for finding that, and thanks—"

"Stop thanking me already. You're my very best friend. Isn't that what best friends are all about? See you at breakfast. Wish it was now. I'm going to dream pancakes tonight. Thousands and thousands of them. 'Bye, Mick."

" 'Bye, J.P. My God," he said, looking at his watch.

"It's eleven thirty. Tomorrow's almost here. I'll see you *soon!*"

"Well, you did it kid," Angelo said. "How do you feel?"

"Great, Ange. Tired out but great."

"I'm proud of you and Lisa. I had a feeling she'd win after I saw her practice last week. She put her all into it, didn't she?"

"She sure did. And how did you like that little girl who won?"

"She was fine, wasn't she? It makes me feel good when I see young talent like that on roller skates. I've spent my whole life in this business. I've seen it at its height and at its lowest. And now I'm seeing it all come back again. It makes me wish I had another fifty years to give. Well, I'd better get on home, too. I've had a long day. You sure you want to lock up Wonder Wheels tonight?" he asked, knowing Mick did.

"You don't mind, Ange?" Mick asked, knowing he didn't.

"Not at all. This place belongs to you as much as it does me. It's in our blood, in our hearts. Despite our ages, we have a lot of things in common. One of them is the love for this old place. Next fall I'm putting a new coat of paint on, and if business keeps going as it has been, I might even get new neons for the marquee outside. That *L* in *WHEELS* is about shot. Good night, kid. Thanks for making me feel so fulfilled."

Mick heard the lock on the front door snap closed. He looked around the empty rink, drinking in the quietness and stillness that felt so good. He rolled onto the floor, skating around the middle of the rink until the 5-P bench caught his eye. He stopped short, stood still, then skated over to it and sat down. Slowly and gently he rubbed his fingers over the edge of the high-polished wood, as if he could command Kitty's presence.

Why? Why? Why? he asked himself. Why, Kitty?

There were times he couldn't accept the fact that she was dead. There were times he expected her to walk into Wonder Wheels again, skate with him, talk and laugh, be close by his side.

He stretched out on the bench, placing his head down on the side where Kitty always sat. His long legs dangled over the other end. He wanted to be alone here in Wonder Wheels tonight. It was his silent, personal way to share it all with Kitty.

He closed his eyes to bring back memories. A collage of thoughts and images fled through his head. He could hear her voice as if she was standing over him:

Me Kitty, you Mick. . . . Want to do nothing together? I'll meet you and we'll just do nothing together. . . . I missed not seeing you skate last

*night. I did. I really did. . . . Being crazy with
you is fun. . . . I never felt spaghetti throb before. . . . I'll be with you each and every moment. Think of me. I love you, Mick Thompson.*

A single tear rolled down his cheek and chin and
onto his neck. He wiped it off with the back of his
hand. He didn't want to cry anymore. He wanted to
think about Kitty without crying. The memories
they shared were so vivid, so beautiful; he only
wanted to think about those.

But he couldn't. Kitty's death had carried life's
merry-go-round a full circle past him—too fast, far
too fast.

He thought and thought until, without realizing
it, he fell asleep on the bench—on *their* bench in
Wonder Wheels.

LEE BENNETT HOPKINS is well-known for his numerous anthologies, picturebooks, professional texts and articles, as well as *Mama*, his first novel for young people.

Mr. Hopkins grew up in Newark, New Jersey, the setting of *Wonder Wheels*, where he was an avid roller skater during his teens. He now lives in Scarborough, New York.